# NEVERHOME

# NEVERHOME

## Laird Hunt

Chatto & Windus
LONDON

Published by Chatto & Windus 2015

First published in the United States by
Little, Brown and Company in 2014

2 4 6 8 10 9 7 5 3 1

First published in Great Britain in 2015 by
Chatto & Windus
Random House, 20 Vauxhall Bridge Road,
London SW1V 2SA

A Penguin Random House Company

Penguin
Random House
UK

www.randomhouse.co.uk

Addresses for companies within The Random House Group Limited can be found at:
www.randomhouse.co.uk/offices.htm

The Random House Group Limited Reg. No. 954009

A CIP catalogue record for this book
is available from the British Library

ISBN 9780701188795

Printed and bound by CPI Group (UK) Ltd, Croydon, CR0 4YY

For my grandmothers and my grandfathers

*A sublime and awful beauty – a fearful and terrible loveliness...*

John Quitman Moore,
*DeBow's Review*, 1861

# ONE

I was strong and he was not, so it was me went to war to defend the Republic. I stepped across the border out of Indiana into Ohio. Twenty dollars, two salt-pork sandwiches, and I took jerky, biscuits, six old apples, fresh underthings, and a blanket too. There was a heat in the air so I walked in my shirtsleeves with my hat pulled low. I wasn't the only one looking to enlist and by and by we had ourselves a band. Farm folk cheered as we went by. Gave us food. Their best shade to stop in. Played to us on their fiddles. Everything you've heard about from the early days, even though it had already been a year since Fort Sumter, and there had already been the First Bull Run, and Shiloh had stole off its souls, and the early days were done and dead and gone.

The tenth or eleventh night on the road we drank whiskey and hollered under the stars. There was a running race. Knife throwing. Cracker-swallowing contest. Feats of strength. One of the boys tried to arm wrestle me and got the back of his hand scraped when I smacked it down. None of the others took a turn.

There was an old lady outside Vandalia fetched me up a drink of water from her well, took a long look at me as she handed it to me, and told me I needed to watch my step. No one else outside that lady saw what I was. I slept just exactly like a pine plank on that walk. I sent Bartholomew my first letter from Dayton. I sent him about the same one from Cincinnati. I wrote that I missed him fierce. I wrote that I was fierce happy too.

I gave my name as Ash Thompson down out of Darke County. 'Where in Darke County?' they asked me, and I told them, even though I could see straight off they weren't listening, that *where* was in the northwest corner of that fine county on my Daddy's farm. After they had cracked on my teeth and whistled at my thick fingers and had me scrape my thumb calluses across the wood tabletop, they gave me my blues. A week later, when they saw I didn't mind work and hadn't run off, they handed me my firearm. It was a Model 1861 muzzle-loading Springfield rifle with flip-up sights and percussion lock, and they said you could use it to kill a man a quarter mile away. That was something to think about. How you could rifle a man down was looking at you and you at him but never see his face. I hadn't figured it that way when I had thought on it back home. I had figured it would be fine big faces firing back and forth at each other, not threads of color off at the horizon. A dance of men and not just their musket balls. There was another fellow, little bitty thing made me look tall, said something not too far off these lines aloud as we stood there staring at our Springfields.

'Don't you worry, sweetheart,' said to him the officer was

handing out the hardware, 'you'll get so close to those rebel boys you won't know whether to kiss or kill.'

We marched ragtag for several days south and came to a great camp near the river. They gave me a shovel to go with my rifle and set me to digging fresh latrines. Some already there had it in their minds my first day to strip me down and throw me in the creek, but one of the band I'd come in with said it wasn't worth the trouble I would give them if they tried it, so they picked on someone else instead. I stood on the bank and laughed with the others when they had him down to his dirty skin, but it was me who waded in when it came out he couldn't swim. I wasn't sorry after I'd fetched him, as the wet and cool settled off some of my stink. That evening I walked a ways down the creek past all the eyes and shucked off my own clothing and went back in. I'd have floated on my back a good long while but I could already see that a camp was a sprawly thing and who knew who else might have had the same idea, so I got in and out and dried and dressed back up quick.

The boys at my tent had a game of cards going when I got back and I stood awhile and watched it. In between bets they talked about all the rebel-whipping to come. They had pipes in their mouths, and cheeks still fat from their farms. I did not know what was coming any better than they did but it did not feel like a thing to rattle happy at the dark about. Still, when one of them looked up from his poor hand and asked how many rebels I planned on killing, I smiled and put

my own pipe in my mouth and said I'd get my hundred. A
little later after I had tended to my gun and polished my bayonet I lay under my blanket and thought about that hundred.
I thought about my Bartholomew too. I thought about the
hundred then I thought about Bartholomew then I fell asleep
and dreamed I was floating dead as the ages in the cool waters
of the creek.

We had talked on it for two months before I went. I think
we both of us knew from the start where the conversation was
wending but we talked on it, took it every angle, sewed at it
until the stitch stayed shut. I was to go and he was to stay.
There was one of us had to look to the farm and one had to go
and that was him and that was me. We were about the same
small size but he was made out of wool and I was made out of
wire. He took the sick headache every winter and I'd never
got sick one gray day in my life. He couldn't see any too well
over a distance and I could shut one eye and shoot a jackrab-
bit out of its ears at fifty yards. He would turn away any time
he could, and I never, ever backed down.

He said we didn't either one of us have to go and I said
someone wasn't him had to go and represent this farm and
after I put the bark on my words and said it a few times that
settled up the argument. We kept it quiet. The only other
person I raised up the topic with was my mother and of course
she was already fine and dead. I would open the discussion
with her after Bartholomew was into his snoring or when we
were at different ends of the field or when it was my turn to go

out to the shed and lay my cheek and shoulder against our cow. Once or twice I went out to the churchyard where I'd put her stone. Curried off its fresh slime and damp mosses and twittered at it like a bird. My mother had traveled in a train once and I told her I wanted to travel like her. Whoosh across the countryside, float the length of its long waters in a boat. I wanted, I told her, to lie under the stars and smell different breezes. I wanted to drink different waters, feel different heats. Stand with my comrades atop the ruin of old ideas. Walk forward with a thousand others. Plant my boot and steel my eye and not run.

I said all this to my dead mother, spoke it down through the dirt: there was a conflagration to come; I wanted to lend it my spark. We both of us, me and Bartholomew, knew what my mother would have said in response and so it was like she was saying it each time I asked her what she thought.

*Go on. Go on and see what you got.*

We had drill every day at that camp. We filled up our bags and toted our muskets and we marched long miles out into nowhere and back and we stood at attention for inspection and spent every second we stood there wishing the hot weather would turn. I finished up at drill and dug at the trenches and at any other thing required a shovel. Once it was a sinkhole for the cooks. Another time it was a row of fresh neat graves I helped dig and then fill. Boys they put in them had died of diphtheria. One or two was ones I had walked into camp with. Five-minute funerals were but one of our many fine diversions. There was stealing and drinking and fighting too. There was a little stage where they would get up farces about the officers or stories I knew well, like the little man could spin gold or that poor boy and girl who laid down their bread crumbs in the woods. I heard one fellow say that since those two got free at the end and didn't get cooked in an oven they were lucky, but there was another said, You get a scare like that put deep into you when you are young, it never comes all the way out.

Whether it does or it doesn't, we also had minstrel shows for our entertainment or actual Negroes free from bondage to dance for us or sing. There was a giant contraband they said had come up out of Tuscaloosa on an earless donkey did his song for us on a platform he had balanced on the top of a fence post. When the song was done he bowed then flipped off that platform backward and onto the ground. He did this so well the boys had him do it again. The third time, when the crowd had swelled up to almost half the regiment, he landed bad off his jump and broke his leg.

It wasn't just contraband could offer up marvels. A Mexican boy worked in the kitchen tents could play the banjo so fast his hand would vanish clear off the strings, and there was plenty said in hushed voices when it came to picking, it was only the devil on his good day had him beat. Some afternoons the officers would get up contests. The whiskey would go around on those days and the boys would run races or fight each other with their bare fists or play a kind of baseball involved old apples we didn't yet know we'd want later or climb up greased poles.

The camp was about as far away as you could gallop in a day from what you would have called a pretty place. There was torn-up pasture fields around us and half the woods cut down for timber and firewood. There was a stink out of a old storybook doing its dance on any breeze might come our way. Men blowing along their own ugly breezes went every which direction, some on horse though most on foot, and there was a little line of cannon they would fire off every now and again when there wasn't enough smoke and devil smell around to suit them. The tents were dark places, for all that the men would lay down floors and hang up likenesses and sundries from home. Sometimes there were women in the camp. But whether they were officers' wives or pot scrubbers or ladies had long ago lost their virtue, I kept clear of them.

When I'd eaten up my given share of a day I'd take up my pen to write Bartholomew. I had never written him or anyone else a letter before those days in my life and I did not much like the look of what I found I had to say. I have improved some at writing since, as you can be the judge, but I was slow at my writing back then and using my pen to make words that would still mean something after traveling so many miles seemed a strange chore. I would read through my letters before I posted them off and it seemed like I was reading the letters of a stranger to a stranger and I did not like the way this made me feel.

*My Dear Bartholomew,*
*Dearest Bartholomew,*
*Bartholomew, My Handsome Friend,*

Back home it was words spoke aloud or little presents and notions we would leave for each other that had done the trick. We had a game between ourselves to be the one to see the first daffodil come up in the springtime, the first tulip, the first iris cracking open the fresh purple yolk of its bloom. Who-ever saw it was to pick that first one and put it out for the other to find. That spring before I left for the fight it was Bartholomew had seen the first lilac. He tied some sprigs into a little bundle with yellow thread and set it out next to my breakfast bowl. I thought on that bright bundle more than once in my writings to see if there was any fair firsts I could signal to him, but all that came into my mind were latrines and ugly bare backs set to labor and burned coffee and mealworms popping their heads out of our hard biscuits. One day on a march I did see a blue heron spear a fish bigger than its beak out of a still puddle but when I wrote it down, the heron and the fish and the puddle came out so pale I almost struck them out.

Bartholomew's letters to me were of another order altogether. He had a way of writing five words could bring all of the old world back to life. Reading his letters I could smell the early smells of autumn and hear the early autumn sounds. One time he put a bright red cardinal feather in the envelope and told about finding it 'aflit at the edge of the well' into which it might have fallen forever had he not plucked it up and sent it to fly far across the world to find me. I cannot tell you quite why but that feather and his words about it flying far to find me put a tear into the corner of my eye wouldn't leave even after I had wiped it away. I wasn't the only one got my face flushed at a letter from home. Some got much worse than that. There was young boys got letters from their mothers who bawled like babies all the rest of the night. One time, I saw an old sergeant sent a pair of fresh-knit socks from his wife had to work hard to bite back the tears. A pair of fellows sitting nearby tried to tease him some but he told them if they kept it up one more minute he would stick a fork in each of their eyes.

It was that same sergeant taught us how to fix bayonets in our Springfields and stab at men made of straw and form a line and, for those that didn't know how already, shoot. I already said earlier I knew how to shoot, and fifty yards or five hundred, it wasn't much different in that camp. I could make my Springfield hit whatever it was they wanted me to wherever they wanted to put it and it didn't matter if they stood behind us while we were at it and yelled in our ears or beat to breaking on a drum. There was plenty who could march or stand longer than I could or stab straw fiercer, but it was only a few could beat me with a gun.

I wrote Bartholomew about it, and in the next letter I had from him he said that was fine and I ought to be proud but that – like we had talked about – if I didn't want the curious eyes of the entire company on me, every once in a while I needed to miss. I wrote him back that maybe it wouldn't be so awful a thing to get noticed for what I was and sent home. He wrote that he wanted me back with him more than anything on the green good earth but that I shouldn't come. That he knew I wasn't ready to come home yet, that if I didn't stay to see some of the fight I would forever be filled with the echoes of regret and the ague of remorse.

There was a fellow had his tent near ours who looked wiser

than the others and I asked him after I had had this letter from Bartholomew whether he thought love ought to trump duty. 'Love? What in hell is love?' said this wise-looking man and spat.

They got us what they thought was trained up enough – to where we wouldn't stab or shoot at each other too much – and we boarded paddleboats and went down the river, then got off and marched toward the fiery South. There was battles up ahead and soon as word got around that we were moving forward to make their acquaintance, the regiment commenced to bleed off a number of its boys. It wasn't anything at all to step away from the line and not come back. A kind of mud and mist covered our faces. We were unknown things that marched along with muskets. We might have done a thing or two back in the camp to get us noticed but now that camp was left behind. The sergeant had seen I could shoot hadn't come along. The boys from my band had seen me at arm wrestling weren't there. I'll confess it to you, is all I'm saying, that I thought about leaving many was the time as we marched. Despite what Bartholomew had written me about my not being ready to come home yet. Despite all I said those days to my dead mother.

'I won't run,' I said to her.

*You will or you won't,* she said back.

'There is no storm of ice or fire can make me run,' I said to her.

*You will learn whether that's a lie one way or the other,* she said back.

I was thinking about it, about leaving and putting the lie straight into my step, when we marched through one of those towns where they were all lined up to cheer and we saw a girl climbing a tree to look at us better. There must have been something sharp on one of the branches because her chemise got caught as she climbed and it tore right off. That brought a roar up out of all the boys around me, and the girl in the tree took the chemise that she wasn't wearing any longer and waved it at us. You could see that she was sorry, even as she waved her torn garment, that she was all of her bouncing in the breeze, and before I knew what I had done I was up the tree like it was a ladder and had taken off my jacket and wrapped it around her. I wrapped it around her, pulled it snug. 'There you go, miss,' I said. I said this and gave a kind of bow even up there in the tree and she looked at me, then she looked at me harder, and she saw what I was and gave a start turned her eyes from blue to green, but then another happy roar come up – this one for what I had done – from the boys below and I got down the tree and back into the line. I saw her wearing my jacket, still looking at me and pointing, but before I'd taken five or ten more breaths the company had moved on and we had left that girl behind.

16

That evening I stood before our Colonel, and after he had given me a week of midnight picket duty for handing away my military issue before I'd even had a chance to get shot at in it he complimented me on my tree-climbing talents and on my gallantry. He said he hadn't known they made farm boys that were acquainted with the fancy arts. He said that the world never ceased to offer him up surprises. That the world was nothing but surprises from one long end of it to the other.

'What surprises *you*, Private Thompson out of Darke County?' he asked me.

'Sir?' I said.

'I asked you what in this wide world of war and its thunders surprises you.'

I had my answer come to me quick but still I thought a long minute or two before giving it.

'Everything, sir.'

The Colonel had the habit of twisting at his mustaches. He twisted first on one side then on the other, then he nodded. He looked at my face awhile and I could tell he was seeing a tree and a jacket and some pretty young woman that wasn't me.

There was good sport on my account that evening at the

17

fires. A boy with some skill at the guitar, an instrument I had never seen played out of doors, had already worked the episode into a tune. ' "Gallant Ash went up the tree, helped a sweet old girl along..." '

That boy didn't have the voice Bartholomew had when he was at his fiddle of an evening when we were sitting together on a straw bale under the stars but I'd heard worse. Another boy could play the bones took up with him. There was some hands clapping. Two or three got up a kind of jig that they pulled me into the middle of and made me hop and shuffle along.

When I went out later to my first night of picket, that song came with me. There was a Louisville boy on duty with me called me Gallant Ash and hummed some of it. I told him he'd better keep that name to himself but some of the others heard and took it up and then there wasn't any stopping it. Even our Colonel, when I saw him again the next day, handed it over at me to wear, so I put it on.

Wearing it the following night I shot my first man. Six or seven of them looking to harass and harry, or Lord knows what, came up out of the trees an inch or two before dawn. Half the boys on our portion of the line were nestled in the leaves and slow to rise so it was only a few of us had our muskets at the ready and fired at the blurs come running through the draw. Only one of our firearms functioned and that was mine. I got a look at the man I'd killed when his brothers had run off. He had curly dark hair and a little beard. His mouth was large and his cheekbones high. The ball had hit him just above his left breast. You could see a kind of brown bloom coming up through his light coat. He had a filthy old dressing on his left hand and fingernails could have used a trim.

Our relief came with the sun and told us to head back and report, but I stayed on a minute with the killed man. Like anyone else, I'd seen plenty of the dead, but never one I had made. I had just that morning crafted another light remark about how many rebels I aimed to account for, how many I planned to shoot and skin. We had larked on that subject every day. Some of those had already been in fights had told us that what we were most likely to do when the enemy was all lined up and aiming at us was run. But I had not run. I had fired my weapon.

'Did you see that, Mother,' I whispered.

*I saw it,* she whispered back.

Now there I sat. I wanted to take up the dead man's head and cradle it but I did not do that and knew that that kind of a thought was another thing I was going to have to learn to kill. Some of them on relief teased me a little as I sat there my minute but I didn't pay them any mind. They hadn't killed anyone that morning. When the sun was up sufficient I saw that the dead man's open eyes were blue.

One week later, the Colonel, whose horses were off working elsewhere, had one of our lieutenants form up a party to search out a likely forward encampment and told him to take me along. It was a dozen of us then to tromp through the trees and creeks, and after living with a thousand it felt like it was just us and the birds left to populate an empty earth. We saw none of the enemy nor any two-leggers white or dark at all. We scouted a ways and struck a deserted house or three but none fit for a camp. The lieutenant had us split ourselves up then to cover more ground and after walking an hour, me and the boy I was with found what looked like the right place hiding away in the trees.

It was a pretty piece of land with a fine, bright stream to split it. There was a stone bridge could take the weight of our guns across it and a cabin for the Colonel and his officers. There was a barn still had straw in it and a big oak tree we sat under a minute to chew our apples and biscuits and a well we pulled good water up out of. Next to the well was a shed. In it we found a chain and a shackle lying open next to a declivity in the dirt floor. You could see the shackle had been shut hard awhile and probably many a time on something soft.

We might have stood on for a bit to look at this sorry spectacle but at that minute a good-size pig that hadn't long been wild come snorting by. We shot the pig, got it trussed and hung on a birch pole between us, and made our way back to the meeting point, where after many a rest we presented our pig and made our report. Turned out some of the others had found a choicer spot and that's where the regiment moved but that didn't stop a good number of us, including the Colonel, from chewing that night on fresh pork.

I wrote Bartholomew about that day and that meal in my next letter to him. I thought about some of the birds I had seen and put those down and about some of the trees and the fine construction of the bridge and the sound of the creek moving under it and included that in my letter too. The pig we had shot had squealed about as loud in its dying as a pig called Cloverleaf we once had back home and I made the comparison in my letter to Bartholomew and reckoned it was true. I read through it after I thought I had finished it enough and hadn't quite ruined up every inch of it and I was getting ready to fold it for sending when that shed came back to me. I saw the shackle and the old blood caked on the iron and gave a shudder. That shudder started somewhere down low in my back and came up through my throat and breached my mouth. There wasn't anyone alive hadn't seen someone with a shackle someplace on his body, I knew that, but there had been a bite of sorrows in that empty place made me glad to think we had found another spot and weren't going to return.

Return I did, though. The very next day the Colonel instructed me and my fellow to lead a forage party to the environs to see if we could scare up another nice piece of pork. I walked us straight there like I had the map to it written on my shirtsleeve. There was as much sun out as there had been the day before and an even better breeze. We killed another pig, and the boys I was with all thought we ought to have set our camp there but I didn't say a word. From a distance the shed, with its door hanging off one of its hinges, looked like it opened up onto a darkness would lead you, if you studied at it too closely, down to a place you would have to work hard to climb your way back up out of.

There was still plenty used my nickname, but I didn't feel any too gallant over the next coming days. I expect if any of the ladies we saw as we marched had lost her shirt to her excitement I'd have let her air out her luxuries in the breeze. Many was the time I stepped off the line to look for a bush and had to trot to catch back up. I wasn't the only one had swallowed up some swamp water at the camp we had chosen and was paying the price. None of us had any interest in squatting down in front of the others and looked to put good distance between us, but the still real prospect of one of them stumbling onto me at my business I was at every ten minutes instead of every ten hours and uncovering my secret didn't help cheer me up. It didn't cheer me up any much more either when a boy came back from his own trip to the bushes carrying a skull in his hand.

Turned out we were walking through where one of the earliest skirmishes had been and some of the fallen had gone unburied and their bones had been scattered by animals and wind. Soon as we learned this we got bones on the brain and for the next mile, green and brown and mossy white was all we could see.

'There's one over there,' someone would say.

Another would call out, 'There's a boot down there at the base of that tree still got some foot stuck in it.'

There were bones in the ditches, bones in the fencerows, bones in the cattails, and bones in a kind of circle at the shallow black bottom of a brook. There was some didn't like all that calling out about bones and thought we ought to stop and do them their justice, regardless of whose they were, blue or gray, but the Colonel had his orders and the regiment was moving and we kept our mouths open and fingers pointing and left our shovels alone.

That feeling of wanting to bury the bones we saw, which had lingered long past the seeing of them, didn't keep the boy with the skull from pulling it out when we tromped some miles later through a little town, nor from tossing it into the hands of a local belle turned out to watch us pass. A number of us gave out a good laugh when he did this. Not the belle. She neither laughed nor shrieked nor dropped the mossy thing but considered it a minute and then turned and set it carefully on the window ledge next to her. I looked at her over my shoulder a little and wondered at how, after that gift, her lips had made themselves into a strong little smile and at how she had met and held the eye of anyone who looked at or spoke to her as we all trooped past. There was a child or two in the shadows behind her. The front of the house was fire-blackened and the roof had been part stove in. My stomach gave a tug and I turned away but I didn't stop thinking about her even when I ran off again to find a quiet spot. Who knew what the skull meant to her and hers. As I squatted there at my business, I tapped a time or two on my own skull to make sure it was still resting there snug on my neck.

$M$y mother had a story she liked to tell about a man heard Death was waiting up around the bend. He changed his direction and walked the other way. You know how that ends. I had known it before I left for war and I knew it down there in the South with its bones and ball-stove roofs, so when the regiment's numbers commenced again to drop after a call to double-time it up to the sound of the cannon we had begun to hear, I gripped harder at my Springfield and swung my cartridge box around behind me and quit my trips to the bushes and followed fast. I did not even start to imagine what it would be like not to follow. I was only sorry that I would be obliged to engage with my stomach in its poor shape. Not so sorry, though, that I slowed when a pair of corporals jogged down the line telling those who were too sick to drop back. Nor did I, nor any of those around me I am proud to say, slow down when the cannon fire grew so hot it seemed like the injury was already being done to us before we had fairly arrived and that we were already part of the world's everlasting grief and glory, and we could see the trees crashing down destroyed in the heights and hear the sound, from all quarters, of hurt men letting the air out of their throats.

We started to see gray off at a distance, just little speckles of it but everywhere, and they had us take off our knapsacks and anything else wouldn't help in the fight. I didn't have time to be sorry to see Bartholomew's likeness and all my letters from him go. I just untangled the sack like all those around me were doing and let it drop. We all but ran then. There was a company of ours up ahead having hell's time and needed our help at holding the flank. I had stood at the picket and fired off my rifle at a man as I've already said, but there's a first time for battles too. Some good number of us fell as we made the last effort, and the air filled itself up with smoke. It seemed like we would never get to where we were going and then we were there.

We had come to a field as long and wide as you like with us on one side and them on the other. It was their boys in their soldier hats and us in ours. If we'd been wearing the same colors, you could have thought it was a mirror. Like the central job of it was we were fixing to fire at ourselves. Like the other half of it, the mirror, was fixing to fire straight back. I got this idea I gripped hard on to that there had to be skirmishers go out first, that we would each send out a wave at each other, that it wasn't yet time for the rest of us to fight. Our Colonel came riding up behind us about then and put that idea right out of my head. He rode up, then got down off his horse and gave his mustaches a twist and said we hadn't come all the way over from Ohio to pick petunias, that it was time to bring thunder, to fling doom, to stand shoulder to shoulder and never fear the dark. While he made this speech the grays kept creeping forward and we did too and when we had both quit creeping our throats and eyes had already started fighting and our colors stood not forty yards apart.

There had been a sutler in camp just the day before had tried to sell off a set of iron armor could keep out, he had said, any bullet built by man and see you home to your loved ones but he had been laughed down. I got a picture of that armor in my head though when the gray volleys commenced and the boy next to me caught his ravishing and fell away just as we were lifting our guns. The boy on the other side of me croaked out about sure wishing he had a rock or tree to stand behind, and the old fellow been in plenty of fights next to him laughed and bit open a cartridge, sniffed loud, and said, 'You are the tree, son.'

I<sub>t</sub> was nothing but marching and battles, marching and double-timing and battles all the long days after that. Once, they put us on a train to take us farther east but I didn't think about the world whooshing by, I just thought about the engine smoke in the cattle car they had us in and the boys couldn't take the rocking and kept getting sick out the open door and a duckling-shaped bruise I had on my rear parts so I couldn't show anyone made it painful to sit. Another time, after we had fought in a swamp had us picking leeches off our everywheres for days, they carried us where they wanted us in a boat sat so low in the water we expected the whole time anything like a wave would come by and Lee's work would be done for him because we would all drown.

Each time we fought we took off our knapsacks and made a pile out of them. It got to where we'd feel the ground shake and start to shrug them off. I lost two knapsacks when the rebels took our ground and I quit carrying my photographs and letters in them. After I lost the second one I had Bartholomew get another likeness made. The likeness-maker mistook Bartholomew's intention, figured him for a boy about to head off for the fight, and had him pose in his tall hat next to a weapon that it came off clear in the likeness Bartholomew wasn't any too comfortable having to grasp. He wrote in the accompanying note that it was a counterfeit worse than any in the Confederacy, but I liked this picture of my soldier wasn't any soldier holding his musket like it was a hot rake or a bear's leg, and after I had looked at it a good long while, I sewed it into the wrappings I wore under my shirt.

I had been shy to send my own picture to him but after all those battles I thought I better get my own likeness taken before I got my ticket to hell or lost an eye or an arm. So I got myself a pass and walked the ten miles up the road to where I could catch a wagon into Washington City. It was my intention to spend the portion of the day I didn't use in likeness-making to see some of the sights of that great city we were all defending, but the wagon I was riding in got stuck when the driver fell asleep and its mules ran it into some deep mud. It took two hours to fetch it out and by the time we reached the outskirts, which was nothing better than a few deserted houses, a kicked-in stable, and tents and cook fires as far as I could see, I knew it was going to be all I could do to make my way back at something like a reasonable hour. So much for sights and seeing. Luckily there was a likeness-maker said he had other likenesses to deliver to my camp when they were ready who had his wagon set up next to a tonic seller down along the banks of the Potomac. Now, there was a fine piece of wet property. I never saw our capital, and expect now I never will, but I saw its river and felt its cool waters, as I put

30

my feet into it while I was waiting for my turn. There was a preacher down by the water hawking his wares too. There were preachers and men just liked to talk and tap a Bible at every turn of the war, and I listened to them about as much or little as anyone else, but this one, down by the waters of the Potomac, had a style to him that went beyond a handsome way to say *Mary, Joseph, and Jeremiah.* I considered a minute letting the fellow behind me skip over me so I could listen a little longer, but the hour was advancing and I had my chore to accomplish.

We never used our bayonets for much of anything but cooking and cutting weeds but the likeness-maker had me hold a hoary old blunderbuss had a bayonet hammered onto it permanent for the photograph. He fussed his way under his cloth and looked through his lens and told me I looked just like a real soldier. My ears were still ringing from the previous week's brawl, and I had seen a fellow from the line cut by balls into five big pieces not three days before.

'I look like a soldier because I've been soldiering, you son-of-a-bitch,' I told him.

'Now, now, gentle down, son' is what he said.

He did his work, though. Give credit where credit is due. I do look something like a real soldier in that piece of tin he had delivered the next day. My jaw was set and my cap sat cockeyed and my eyes were as wild as a snakebit colt's. Bartholomew wrote me when he received it that he had sewn a smart case for it out of some soft lamb leather but that he had not yet dared to look too directly at it for fear that the likeness would shove aside the sweet memory he kept of me.

'Look at it after they have killed me, then,' I wrote him, for I had a pique on me that he would not look at my picture I'd worked a day at to get made for him.

'If they kill you I will sew it up in its case forever and bury it with my heart in the yard,' he wrote me.

'Well, in the meantime,' I wrote him, 'just take a peek at it and see what you think about how straight they've taught me to stand.'

It wasn't just the fighting they wanted us for. At any quiet moments, they had us help with laying breastworks, with building bridges and cutting logs for their corduroy roads. In the big camps, you found yourself sweating under the sun next to every kind of man there was on this earth. I stripped trees with a red Indian out of New York State had green and purple tattoo stripes up and down his legs and arms, and I carried rocks and wrestled oxen and butchered goats and cleaned cannon and loaded wagons with the sad flesh of soon-to-be corpses next to Chinamen couldn't speak English and Chinamen could speak it better than me and sundry coloreds of all shape, shine, and shade. I think if I had walked straight off the farm and into that work I would have wept at the shock. But the weeks and months had stretched me out into it. You stand in a line in your bright blues with your filthy face and your lice and all the dead you now know and get shot at regular, your thinking takes a change. You get to where you can do things you couldn't have dreamed up the outline of before.

'Pick up that pile of arms'; 'Shoot that line of horses'; 'Kill anything that moves. Kill anything that doesn't' came the orders from my lieutenants and my captains and my Colonel and any other wore the right uniform. You followed them, simple as that, and if you didn't follow them when the fighting was hot, you died. Maybe you died anyway. There was always that. Death was the underclothing we all wore.

'Charge those cannons' came the order. 'Kick their fucking teeth out.' 'Break his other leg.' 'Don't you let them leave.' 'Burn them up alive.' After it had gone on awhile, if they had told me to dig a hole, jump in it, and carry their colors down to hell, I would have dropped my pack and tried.

What I wasn't ready for came when they had a regular troop of contraband in to help us near Sharpsburg. This group had been cut to pieces by fierce fire and had saved a hospital full of our wounded boys went the story, and they lived as you could see on half our poor rations without a grumble and we gave them their respect. We worked alongside them for several days and then they got the call to go to help out elsewhere. It was when they were formed up and starting to walk out that I saw a worker in their number wasn't like the others. This worker was long of leg and broad of shoulder and carried an ax could have cut down a redwood tree. The worker looked at me, got lit up in the eyes, and nodded as their line went past.

'Hey, you,' I called out.

'Hey, you, your own self,' she called back.

I had dreams of getting seen and discharged in disgrace every night the next week after that. I wrote down this dream to Bartholomew and sent it to him and he sent me back a letter said he had had his own dream. In it I had come back home crazy from the fight. I worked the farm but couldn't speak plain English anymore. I dug at the ground with my gun and was bleeding all over and couldn't quit that bleeding no matter how many poultices he applied.

He sent me a thimble of dirt in that letter and asked me to swallow it so I could remember him and our good old home. I wrote him back that I remembered him and it and that I didn't do anything but that all the time. I wrote him that I thought sometimes I might die if I did not see him soon, that it made me homesick unto my death when I considered how I might be shot down and never see him nor the farm again. I wrote him, as I had written him before, that I kept his likeness sewed tight to my breast and that I touched at it every night before I slept. I wrote him that if it was crazy to think I might die of the thought of us never again getting to sit quiet together – holding hands or not, just sitting, being back there like we had always been, on our chairs or hay piles in the yard – then I was crazy and they ought to take away my hat and my rifle and feed me to the hogs.

I wrote him all of this. Then saw that I was shaking and shivering at the end of it. When one of my tent mates asked me what was wrong I told him he could go to hell. When he was gone I took the dirt Bartholomew had sent me and swallowed it straight down.

I had that dirt in my stomach when the Colonel called at my tent earlier than I liked the next morning and stood outside quietly coughing a minute while I clambered up out of my blankets and stepped over my fellow sleepers and tugged on my shoes.

'I hear there are fat squirrels in those woods, Gallant Ash,' he said when I was up and out in front of him with my jacket pulled half on.

'Yes, sir, I have heard the same,' I said.

'Heard or seen?' he said.

'Seen,' I said, then added, 'There's lots of them,' though I wasn't sure at that minute whether or not any part of this was true.

'Well, I have a cook, this fellow here,' he said, pointing at a cinnamon-colored man with a snowy beard was holding a brace of good-looking hunting metal, 'who claims if I can come up with the substance, he can make me a fine squirrel stew. You think we can come up with the substance?'

'I have shot squirrel before.'

'I would have laid down money on it.'

We carried our weaponry through the still dark and

headed straight for the deeper portion of the woods. We had to go a good ways because everyone in the regiment had made firing into the trees for dinner meat his de facto religion. It was the Colonel who led the walk and who used this choice phrase, *de facto,* and explained to me what it meant.

'So you can say a thing is one way all you want but *de facto* means it's the other,' I said.

'*De facto* is the way it actually is.'

'Are we losing this war or winning it?'

The Colonel let the quiet of the morning answer a while at my question that hadn't had anything close to do with what we were just talking about. Then he let the small cigar he pulled out of his pocket and nibbled the end off of and lit answer at it some more.

'You can still shoot squirrel even if I'm smoking, can't you?' he said.

'Aren't you planning on shooting any yourself?'

'I don't see too well at a distance, especially not in a low light.'

I almost at that minute told him that my husband suffered from the same affliction, came only a thin string away from uttering it. Stood looking down but leaning backward at the precipice.

'Yes,' I said.

'Yes what?' he said.

'I can shoot squirrel and you still smoke.'

I did. Three of them, silver as glittery snakes, two good-size.

I took them all through the head near their nests while the Colonel sat on one log after another with his cigar. After the first one fell near fifty yards off from where we were situated, he apologized for not having brought along a dog.

'I never did hunt with a dog,' I said.

'I always have. When my eyes were still adequate I used to hunt for duck and other waterfowl. Dogs were indispensable. We are short on good dogs in this regiment.'

'I have seen dogs swim but never had one that much liked to.'

'On your farm in Darke County?'

'That's not really where I'm from.'

'Isn't it?'

I looked away from him and deeper into the trees. Felt him shrug. Waited for him to say something else about it but he just sat there, quiet, peering at me with those eyes he'd said didn't work too well.

'Sir, will it make a difference? Does it make any difference?' I said.

'That you are not from where you claimed to come from when you enlisted?'

I nodded.

'I have at least two officers who are not from the cities they claim in their paperwork to have a connection to. I can offer only gross conjecture when it comes to the numbers among the enlisted men. I expect many who have died in our fights together weren't from where they said they were.'

'I'm from another state altogether, I said.'

'All right,' he said, then added. 'As long as it isn't a Southern state. Although now as I say it, I don't know why that would matter. If you are loyal of heart.'

'I am loyal of heart,' I said.

'I know it,' he said after a minute.

'I'm from Indiana.'

'Our good brother to the west.'

'I had my reasons.'

'I'm sure you did.'

'If I die, you might let them know about it in Randolph County, Indiana.'

'At the Thompson farm?'

'Yes, sir, if it weren't too much trouble.'

'I expect it wouldn't be. But let's all hold off on dying.'

'How do we do that, sir?'

He shook his head, smiled a little, then sucked in good and long on his cigar.

'Do you want me to clean these?' I asked.

It took him a minute to know what it was I was talking about, like he had gone off a long way into thoughts didn't necessarily include me and had to journey back to the squirrels and woods to make me my answer.

'The cook can do it. In fact, he told me expressly not to let anyone besides him get anywhere near them with a sharpened knife.'

'All right,' I said.

'Yes, it is all right, Gallant Ash.'

We were in an airy place, a clearing amidst the darker reaches of walnut and hickory and loblolly pine. There were orioles and sparrows at early-morning play in the trees and a breeze carrying through the side-lit trunks could have made you believe it wasn't fixing any second now to get good and hot. At home I had hunted once a week even in winter but I had not picked up a gun to fire at anything wasn't a human being since the Colonel had sent me out after that extra pig. When he handed me one of his small cigars I took it and let him fetch me a light and sat there and breathed air and smoke and felt the dirt from the night before that I had stirred up in talking about Indiana settle back in my stomach. After a while we strung up the handsome squirrels I had shot and talked some more about hunting dogs, then returned to camp.

The Colonel sighed a long loud sigh after we had reached his quarters and he had thanked me for my company and we had handed over the squirrels and our fine rifles to the Colonel's cook. I wanted to ask him what made him sigh so loud but there are some questions you don't get to ask and our walk together was done. Also the cook, with some stage flair, sniffed at the barrels of the rifles we had handed him and rolled his eyeballs in the direction of the Colonel once his nostrils had completed their inspection of the unfired one. When the cook had finished this pantomime, which the Colonel acknowledged with one raised gray eyebrow only, he took up a knife and set to work on the squirrels with such fierce devotion to the chore that neither one of us could take our eyes off him. Later that afternoon, just like the Colonel promised me when I parted ways with him, I found a covered bowl of stew had my name on it sitting on a crack-legged stool outside my tent. I don't know why I took it into my head to tote that bowl off away into the woods to eat. To sit alone in the dusk light next to a holly bush, bats and owls beginning to scar the air above my head, and sup slowly on that stew that tasted better by far than dirt.

You eat dirt, you dream strange dreams. Going-home dreams, dreams in which you try to run across your own fresh-plowed field in pants or dress either one and you can't; in which, home at last, you try to work your own front-door latch and you can't make it budge. You eat handsome-cooked squirrel stew sent over to you by your Colonel, you don't dream at all. Is the way I experienced it. Dead as a dark day to the world and slow to rise again. Fact it took a solid kick to my side applied by the tent mate I had told to go to hell to rouse me. He grinned and nodded when I thanked him for it. He didn't grin as much when I punched him, good and hard, at the meaty part at the top of his arm.

A few hours later, still feeling that long, syrupy sleep, I got captured. I was out on the scatter end of a picket with a couple of greenhorns conscripted out of Akron to keep us new company and who couldn't keep their gums from flapping. It was Longstreet this and Sherman that and they had seen Grant one time in a parade and come autumn Lincoln was going to fall and some sniper man needed to set his sights on Jefferson Davis and put an end to the whole shooting match. They talked up the 'Battle Hymn of the Republic' and said they wished they could dream up a piece of poetry like that, that Madame Julia Ward Howe deserved a place up in the heavens amongst the highest angels for finding such handsome words. They had opinions on our supply lines that were based on information had ceased to be valid back in 1861 and they didn't mind a smidge, maybe even liked it for all I knew, when I corrected them on it. Dark-colored folks were just fine with them because they had seen a pair of impressive ones playing clown and strongman in a traveling show outside Bowling Green one time.

They thought that fighting to free the man in bondage was just about as admirable an occupation as anyone could cook up based on this one long-ago sighting they had probably seen wrong. It rained a lot where they came from, but it was good Northern rain and never made your feet rot. Barefoot fighting was best, they said, but they wouldn't give their shoes away. You gave up your shoes and you were as lost as a soul gone off to his ravishing in a gray uniform. A lassie had shown them her underskirts in Cincinnati on the way to the war. The underskirts had been whiter, is the way they put it to me as we stood out there on picket duty, than the whitest clouds and I thought to myself, my own sad underthings in mind, that she hadn't been wearing them long.

The day before this parley, they had got hold of some fair-quality tobacco, and they took turnabout chewing and spitting and loading up their pipes. I still had the taste of the Colonel's cigar in my nose and I thanked them kindly but declined when they offered me some. I think they had seen about a quarter ounce of engagement between them. About every half of the hour they would interrupt their fine flow of conversation to ask me what I thought, but I told them if I did think, and I tried not to, especially after I had gotten some good sleep, it wasn't their kind of cowpatties I did my thinking about.

They reckoned, I suppose, that this was just salty-veteran talk, which it was and it wasn't, and kept right on airing their opinions and relating their anecdotes. They tried to bring up the Gallant Ash story, which someone or other at camp had thought to revive even though I might as well have climbed that tree and draped that jacket a hundred and twenty years before. I told them there hadn't been anything to it, so they asked me if it was true I had two weeks before, at the greatest risk to my health and happiness, taken cartridge sacks off dead and wounded soldiers in the middle of a fight because my company had shot itself out of ammunition, and I asked them who had told them that. Everyone, they said, was saying it, and they wanted to know if it was true. It was true, I said, I supposed. Then we got taken. The rebel boys, or that's what we first took them for, had just walked right up behind our afternoon parley and poked at us with their guns. I felt so stupid and so angry I about threw up but one of them hit me a handsome one with the butt of his sidearm and told me there wasn't any time for that.

They marched us or kept us standing for the next several hours and it was clear a few minutes into this outing that we hadn't got ourselves taken by regulars but by common out-laws. They told us they knew some rebel captain or major who had promised up a reward for captured Union soldiers. I asked them what this fine officer's name was and what regi-ment he was attached to and what fights he had fought and what fights they had fought and got a fist put hard to the side of my head. They had hiked a good way out from wherever this bounty was. They had come so far from that reward, in fact, that we had to stop halfway there to rest up for the night.

It was in a house looked to have once been nice and wasn't anymore. There was mud streaked on the floors and on the tabletops, and broken crockery lay scattered about. Pages from newspapers and illustrated magazines had been tacked up to the walls then torn off and others tacked up. In one cor-ner, under a cracked sconce, lay what looked like it had once been a vase and the crisped stalks of its former flowers. In another corner lay a pile of grease-stained rebel caps and grays. It didn't add to the smell of the place that one or both of the Akron boys had wet himself when for part of the march after I had spoken, the outlaws had talked about the bounty being 'dead or alive' or 'tortured and dead' or some mix of them both. There was a side room led directly off the main one and after they had given us each another smack and greeted with a laugh and a boot my request for a sip of water they pushed us in and locked the door.

Both those Akron boys, who looked in the smudge of green moonlight we had in there to be no older than sixteen and probably weren't even that, commenced to gibbering as soon as the door had been shut, but I got up and looked out the little window. One of our captor friends was outside leaning against a magnolia tree and smoking a pipe you could see was too fancy by about a half acre not to have been stolen. He looked at me, nodded, took the fancy pipe out of his mouth, and smiled an ugly, brown-gum, gap-tooth smile. He was the one had hit me with his pistol at the start of things and laughed it up the loudest about our drink.

'Why don't you boys climb out the window and suck some fresh air out of my firearm,' he said.

I had already seen up too close that he carried a Colt. Mean-looking piece. Probably special-bore.

'I'll take my chances in here,' I said.

'Wise choice,' he said.

'What is it you plan on doing with us?'

'Turn you in for bounty. You already been told that,' he said.

'Turn us in as what?'

46

He didn't answer, just tapped a little at his boot with the Colt. I could see he was provisioned up with a clay jug. I smiled back at him.

'You enjoy your night now,' he said.

Growing up, I had known a son-of-a-bitch cut about like him lived in the first town over from our farm. I'd see him when we went in for market days. Each time we went in he gave me a lick. Once he pushed me down into a puddle turned the front of my clothes dark brown. My mother was still alive then. Still strong. She looked at me when I walked up to her and shook her head. She worked awhile at selling the corn she had brought and then she turned and grabbed me good by my ear and whispered into it hard.

'We do not ever turn our cheek.'

I looked at that son-of-a-bitch out smoking his stolen pipe by his borrowed tree one more time, then turned away. I went over and leaned against the door that had been locked and saw that it was solid and would not easily be breached. Anyways, there were two of them had their own kinds of pistol were eating at some pork-and-cracker sandwiches they had brandished about for us to admire in the room beyond. There was no gap in the ceiling and none in the floor. There was, though, another smaller door in the room. It didn't open directly onto our deliverance but deliverance offers itself in different ways. It was a narrow closet, the contents of which, lying there like last Sunday's lunch, were made out of felt and crinoline.

47

I have often wondered what my mother would have looked like in a pair of britches. I have tried to pull pants on her legs in my mind but the exercise is not easy; the result does not satisfy. I get them pulled on and think I have done the chore but look again and see that she still has her old brown work dress on. I do know that my mother had legs made of iron and that they were long, and the times I saw them bare they looked like they were holding themselves still and springy at the bottom of a rushing stream. I saw her legs those Sundays of the month we would take our bath. She would step out of the bath and those legs just kept on coming out of the water like they were tornadoes climbing up out of a pond.

I saw boys in the war had legs some like hers but you wouldn't have traded hers for theirs. There wasn't ever anything I saw she couldn't lift if she got her legs under it. Her arms weren't any too thin but it was the legs on her that set her apart. She talked about britches some. We'd have a hired man now and again to help at a chore and we would sit down to lunch and she would chew on her cucumber salad and squint and remark that if the hired man had stacked more hay or climbed a ladder more quickly than she had, it was

48

because he didn't have skirts to get tripped up on. One of these times she told me about how her mother had one whole summer risen up every night and put on her father's work pants and cinched the waist and gone out to do moonlight work on her roses. We did not have any pair of britches in our house but after this story I borrowed a pair off a line outside town and when my mother was asleep one night tugged them on. It was a close night and I did not at all like the feel of the rough wool on my legs but I jumped a puddle and climbed a fence and understood the principle quick enough.

After we had decided that I would go to war, I made a pair of pants out of sackcloth and again went out in the moonlight to practice in them. This time I went out in my britches after dark not because I feared the comment of others but because I did not want anyone beyond Bartholomew to know what I was planning, didn't want anyone to puzzle on it, to speculate. There was and are plenty around could put two and two together and not get nervous to see the sum come out as five.

A time or two of my moonlight parades, Bartholomew came out into the dark with me. We ran barefoot races through the rows. We took a turn at what we thought marching might be and stepped together across the yard. We went scampering down the lane and one night climbed all the trees in the grove. It didn't strike me a second on that night that I might one day think about doing just exactly the opposite, think about taking off my pants and putting on a dress and going out to gain advantage in the dark.

There was no place for dresses that night back home. After we had done our climbing and racing, Bartholomew and I shucked off our britches both of us and lay down together at the edge of our yard. There were mosquitoes out in some number but we thrashed and rolled so eagerly that they barely got a chance at us. Bartholomew came up close on his completion and told me he wanted to stay. 'Stay close now,' he said. But I didn't. I wouldn't. I pushed him away. Saw his fine face in the dark. We had done our trying I told him and look what had come of it.

'I do not want you to leave,' he said.

'Don't you?' I said.

'Constance,' he said.

'Ash, love,' I said, already knowing what to be called.

'You are my Constance,' he said.

'Ash is my name. I will not answer now to any other.'

And when I saw he had no reply to make and wasn't going to get up, only lie there in the yard in his mosquito-bait nothings, I got up myself and pulled on my pants and pushed him aside, a little harder than I like to think of now. Then I went running off away from him, speeding up and slowing down until I felt sure it was starting to come natural and there wouldn't be anything could stop me, like it was to be running races and fence-jumping and tree-climbing from one end to the other of the war.

The son-of-a-bitch with the Colt was drowsing and the Akron boys were asleep and tucked safe away from their troubles a minute in their dreams when I pulled that pile out of the closet and saw that it would do. It was two dresses, one green, one red, owned once by a stout lady gone down the road or into the earth or who knew where. I picked the darkest corner, shrugged out of my clothes and unwrapped myself, and put the green dress on. It was snug in the chest and loose in the waist but I unstrung my belt off my britches and gave it a shape. There was some stain on it but the stain would work to my favor. I tore a stretch of the other dress off and wrapped it around my shoulders in the idea it might approximate a shawl.

Then I drew up the little window, dropped my blues down soft onto the ground, and climbed out. First thing I did was make my way to the bushes where I hadn't gotten to go in what felt like a week. I sat there with that dress on and did my business and a shiver came up over me. I hadn't felt my legs free under a dress in a year, hadn't even so much as held a piece of crinoline let alone have it crawl all over me. I got prickly bumps up to their ends. That image of my mother's legs unspringing

51

themselves out of her bath came back to me. Tornadoes coming up out of the waters. I imagined I had tornadoes under my skirt when I went rustling over in that stout lady's dress to where that son-of-a-bitch lay sleeping his own evil sleep next to the magnolia tree. He had that clay jug on the ground next to him that I had watched him sip out of until he nodded. I picked it up slow then dropped my knee hard onto his chest so that his head popped up and as it did I smashed that heavy jug down. I smashed it down again, and then a third time, and then I put my hand into the blood I had made and brought it back up to my face. I brought some more of it up to my neck, then stood and draped my shawl over my head. Then I took his fine pistol, checked it, cocked the hammer, held it behind my back, and walked around to the front door.

It didn't take but a minute to rouse them. Like I thought it might happen, one of them leaned up at the front window and took a look at me and when he saw me he gave a grin. His teeth didn't look any better than his dead son-of-a-bitch friend's. I said I had been set upon by rogues in the forest, that I needed his help. He opened the door and called me 'honey doll' and I shot him in the mouth. His friend had his gun to hand and he lifted it but got stuck a second too long wondering what it was was happening. What this woman wearing the face of one of their prizes was doing shooting people dead. He took his first bullet in the neck. When he stood and tried a step sideways I put one in his chest. He fell over in the pile of rebel grays. You almost couldn't hear him land. I went over to see if I had finished my work, saw I hadn't, and shot him again.

I put the fine Colt pistol down on the table, then stepped out the front door. I stood a minute and looked down the pale lane ran away off into the dark. Looked like a thought you'd had and then lost. After I had stood I sat down on the front steps. Exactly what Bartholomew had done, the morning I set out on the road that had taken its many windings and had now led me down this pale lane and again into a dress. I had had it in mind that morning of my leaving that despite our troubles of the past year he would give me some fine Bartholomew word of parting, then wave at me as he wiped away a tear. Would stand tall and wave. Instead, he had looked one last time at me, wrapped his arms hard around his chest like he was afraid his lungs might leave him, and sat down.

'You had better get to marching because I can't stand it to see you any longer when you are already gone,' he said when I came over.

'I am not gone yet, husband,' I said.

'Constance is gone,' he said.

He had a far-off look in his eyes, like he had to see through a thousand miles even then, when I was standing right next to him, to find me.

'I am here,' I whispered, bending close.

'Off to war with you, Ash Thompson,' he said.

He said, 'I will stay behind and guard this life we don't have and this family we don't got.'

'Husband,' I said.

'Go on now, Ash,' he said.

He was still holding his arms tight around his chest and not looking in my direction when I rounded the bend.

Now, when I could undouble my own self, I sat down on the front step and wiped at my eyes and thought about my Bartholomew gone from me all those long months and miles away. Then I stepped back in, took up one of the canteens sitting in a slosh on the floor, and drank. The Akron boys had been quiet first but now they were pounding on the door. I drank some more then took off the stout lady's dress, hid it away, wrapped myself back down, got my blues on, picked up some of the dry pork the outlaws hadn't eaten, took a crunch, then let my fellow soldiers out.

'How did you do it?' they asked me when they had had their drink and quit their jumping up and down.

'Trickery,' I told them. 'Trickery simple and pure.'

'There was a lady here,' they said. 'We saw her setting around to the front of the house.'

'Lady?' I said.

They both of them looked at me and I didn't like the way they were looking so I fetched them up a piece of pork each and then, with the fine Colt I had picked back up without knowing why, pointed at the pile of grays serving as a bed to the dead man in the corner.

'You know what they were planning to do with us?' I said.

They shook their heads.

54

'They were planning to put us in those goddamn rebel colors and march us up to their ranks as deserters. I expect when we got close enough they were going to set us loose to run.'

'Why?' they said.

'So that after they had shot us in the back we couldn't answer any questions when they turned us in for deserter bounty.'

It got quiet in that house after I said that and we all stood and chewed and looked at the dead men at our feet and then one or the other of them asked if that was truly what they had planned and I told them I expected it was. As they chewed on and thought about this and gave out a shiver, I told them I didn't want to hear any more talk about ladies walking around the yard. They could tell all they liked about what we had gone through and add whatever they liked about their own hands in our escape. They were thinking about getting candied up as rebels and being shot for deserters and when I said this their eyes went wide and they nodded at the idea of looking like more than spare valises in the closet in the story to be told.

'No more talk about ladies in the moonlight, now,' I said solemnly. They said they felt sure they'd been dreaming and I told them to help themselves to whatever they liked from our friends. One took a rubber cape hung on a chair and the other of them went around the back of the house and borrowed the brogans off the first one I'd killed. They both, 'to show the boys back at camp,' picked up a souvenir firearm. They asked me, greedy-like, if I planned on keeping the Colt. Afraid of where its remaining bullets might take it upon themselves to travel, I told them I thought it ought to stay behind at the scene of its triumph. They smiled and nodded and looked, each one of them, like they were at home and heading back to the nursery for a long sleep. I set the Colt down in the corner amongst the dead flowers and was relieved to no longer be holding it. The outlaws had set our Springfields and cartridge bags by the door to the kitchen and we picked them up. On the way out one of us, might have been me, knocked over the last lit lamp in the house. Instead of putting our boots to the fire we walked on away and let it burn.

In the old days there were Indians here. Miami, Illini, who knows, maybe it was some of the Shawnee. They had a camp on the rise sits in the middle of the front field. Every now and again I still churn up an arrowhead. There are oyster shells from far-off waters in our dirt. There are chiseled bear and wolf bones. When I was a child and my mother let me go, I used to run out to the rise with a feather band on my head. I expect I got a friend or two to play at it with me over the years. You can't pick anything up out of the dirt that will take you close to the true past, but the child a-dance at dusk amid the chopped-down cornstalks can conjure it. That child I was is long gone but I remember some of her tricks and now and again I pick up a lost feather in the yard and feel a flicker. The fields look to move then. The air gets heavy and fills itself with fires and hurt faces.

My mother came to this place when she was a girl. She had grown up a ways near Noblesville, daughter to a blacksmith and the lady who wore pants in the rose garden. The black-smith did well and my mother got a good start on growing up. When I was a child there was a painting of my mother sitting in a carriage next to her father. I do not know if it was

57

her mother made the picture or someone else. Many was the time I would take that painting down off the fireplace and study it. I had never in my life seen my mother in a white dress and I had never seen a bow in her hair. She knew what crinoline felt like. She knew about crepe and silk and every kind of fancy cloth. The horse they had in front of them was a good one, and the blacksmith had his gentle eye on my mother in her white dress and he was smiling. A nice smile. Kind you could linger in. He was a blacksmith come over from the Old Country could read, and he and the lady who liked roses made sure my mother could too. Filled her head with fairy tales. Kind that can make your blood curdle. I still have some of the books they taught her with. He and the lady who liked roses died before my mother was done growing up, and she got sent, her and her books and her picture, to live with an aunt on this farm.

I don't know what happened to my mother's mother, nor do I have much of any idea where that picture is now. What I do know is that when my mother was grown up and had had me and all that was past and she could sit on her own front porch and laugh again her own laugh, she would still dream to waking at night about thorns.

I have my own kind of dream that chases me up and off my bed. In it, I am in the middle of a crowd of faces I ought to know but can't recognize. I have grown small again and can't fight my way through them. It is summertime and the air is close and I need to get to my mother and can't. There is some in the crowd carrying torches. They are talking, loud, but I don't need to hear them to know what they say. I know what they mean to do. I have been here before. The crowd is men and women both. It is a good long time ago. Once not too far back I must have yelled my way half up out of this dream because when I woke, Bartholomew was standing in my doorway looking at me. He stood there and I lay there and then he smiled that small smile of his and went floating back to his bed.

It was that dream came to mind as we stood a minute watching that house start to go up. I get a shiver when it comes and I got a shiver that night so I told the boys we had to go.

'Pretty, ain't it?' one of them said.

'There's dead souls in there,' I said.

They both of them gave a look showed they hadn't thought of that aspect to the equation, then turned to make tracks. Away from the house along the pale lane we hurried. When we came to a road we took it. There were hoot owls in the high branches, sharp-tooth hunters in the trees. We came to a narrow crossroads had a darkened house at each of its corners. There was a white cat sitting on the porch railing of one of them but other sign of life there was none. A half mile up the road we struck a dead mule. It was reclining on its side and had had most of its stomach and much of its front legs chewed off. We passed a pond had the moon painted on its middle. You could see moths diving at it, hoping their hope of the ages about reaching the light. We hadn't got much beyond that pond when we struck a horseman coming through the woods. We all three of us dropped down on one knee and raised our weapons but the horseman held up his hand.

'Union officer, men,' he said.

'Prove it,' one of the Akron boys said.

'Not sure I can, least not to your satisfaction, but if you lower your weapons I'll climb down off Rosie here and we can step off the road and talk.'

We all three looked at each other, then I nodded and they nodded and the horseman kicked his leg over nice and neat and slid down off his mount. He walked him over to a hickory stump, hitched him tight, then told us to come on over and take a seat. There was a mossy log or two shone blue beside him in the moonlight. We came over and sat with him and he pulled out a bottle freshly filled with whiskey. He pulled the cork out with his teeth, took a drink, then offered it over to us. At first I shook my head but he insisted.

'You have that look about you,' he said.

'What look?'

'Of men just been fighting some fight.'

His name, he said, was Thomas Lord and he was a junior cavalry officer attached to the Kentucky Volunteers. He had gotten separated from his unit in a skirmish and now couldn't get his way straight in the dark.

'My horse knows, I just don't trust him as well as I should,' he said.

'That's a fine horse,' I said.

'I rode him to war and haven't stopped riding him and reckon one day, Heaven willing, I'll ride him home.'

'But you don't trust him.'

'It's a defect in my personality. Not the biggest one.'

The horse whinnied when he said this. Lord leaned over and gave him a tender smack on his side. We had broken out the pork and crackers we had taken off the dead outlaws and after he had had a few crunches of what we shared out to him, Lord gave what was left of his part to the horse. The horse ate his portion with his dainty horse lips then shut his eyes. The Akron boys took this for a signal and shut their own and soon were snoring snores that sounded like they had each one shoved a fat frog down his throat. Me and Lord drank awhile and listened to their frogs croak, then Lord asked me what we had gotten ourselves into. I told him. The version where I hadn't done it all. Killed them all. Or put on a dress.

'I heard about schemes like that,' he said. 'There's other varieties but that's the general idea. Especially the part about you ending up in rebel grays and dead.'

'That we got taken in the first place was my fault. I let these two cobs of corn get to carrying on.'

We drank in silence a time. Lord's horse gave out a kind of bark in his sleep and Lord said, 'He's having that dream.'

Like I said, I had been thinking about my own dream, so I gave a look over at Lord. He saw this look and smiled back at me.

'You sit on something long enough you start to be that thing and it starts to be you. I had an uncle in Louisville about never left his soft chair. He would get up and I wasn't the only one would have sworn that chair would give out a cough and wet wheeze just like the ones my uncle did.'

'You are speaking in originalities,' I said.

'My horse is dreaming about a bullet we both of us took.'

I guessed the whiskey had worked up the swirl of war in him and when that happened you couldn't know what a man would say. I met a man in the days after Antietam would drink whiskey then pull out a knife and start to working its point into himself. And not an hour before I had worn a dress and shot two men and killed another with a clay jug to the head. A man telling me what his horse was dreaming seemed small next to that. I leaned back against my stump and nodded and told him to go on.

'We were behind lines, not more than a few slippery feet from Memphis and enough fresh rebels to put the fear into any size mountain of our men. We were not to engage at any cost, was our strict order, just reconnoiter and return to tell the tale. And it looked like we might get the errand done. Happy thinking. The kind has paved many a road down to its doom. Our way out of there took us through an ambush of sharpshooters and in the first volley half our boys got shot. It was a night darker and stranger than this one with winds running hither and thither and the moon playing hide-and-seek in the clouds. You thought you had a line on where they were firing from and then you would know – because another of us had been dropped – that you were wrong. A rumor got started it was Pickett and his boys we were brawling with and that set the strange weather to working in our heads and we started doing even worse than we already had. I don't know how it happened but Rosie and I got ourselves about out of there and up onto a rise. I had one of my boys behind me and raised my hand to signal him to hold a minute when I felt a pinch and saw a musket ball had come to its clattery end in the crook of my fingers.'

Lord held up his hand and pointed to the crook between his third and fourth fingers. Then he traced a line that dribbled down the back of his hand, along his sleeve and went curling into a drop off his forearm.

'As I watched, that bullet slipped out from between my fingers and went falling away. It hit Rosie on his neck before it fell down to the ground. He gave up a shout and reared up like he had been hit for good when he felt it. We both about went over backward onto a pile of rock. In the dream he just had it was him caught the bullet in his right front hoof. And me the one went rearing up.'

'Well, well,' I said.

'That very night when I made my report at camp my commanding officer told me his grandfather had taken a spent bullet better than mine back in 1812. He had taken it directly between the eyebrows with enough fire left in it to penetrate the skin, skid down inside the right side of his face, and lodge behind his ear. When he was a boy, my commanding officer told me, it was a special treat to climb onto his grandfather's lap and take a feel at the nub of bullet buried under his ear skin.'

'That's quite a dream,' I said. Though whether or not I said it out loud was a question. The events of the long day and now this strange colloquy had done their work and I had got settled down, alongside the Akron boys and Lord's horse, into my own froggy snores. Whether Lord joined us awhile I don't know because when we all three woke the next morning he was gone. For whatever reason we did not speak about that meeting as we set out again, and by and by it came to seem to me as vague as the horse's dream.

I had this idea we would march more or less back the way we had come and get ourselves home to camp by suppertime but during our overnight, the scatterings of Secesh forces had swollen up. From a rise we could see them spread out like moldy cauliflower across the valley we needed to traverse so we set off through the soldier pines to make our way around. It was cheerful weather for a hike. There were bluebirds in the green trees and breezes blowing quiet, happy things about. Made the night before seem another world entirely, nothing but twists of whiskey and steam. The Akron boys had been clammed up tight all morning but by and by they started into their chirping again. I expect I joined them for a chirp or two and who knows but what we might have started in with some full-out singing if an hour into our hike we hadn't found ourselves walking through the dead.

It was a shallow grave cut for hundreds hadn't had much of its top put on. There was dust and swirls of leaves blown atop them so that we were several yards in when we realized what it was we had stumbled upon. I had my foot on a hand when one of the Akron boys said, 'I just saw a face.' The other said, 'That down there looks like an arm.' I thought at first it was just Union dead but then I saw there was plenty of gray had joined in too. There was dead and the bones of the dead for the next mile after that. 'Here we go now, boys,' I said. There was dead sitting against trees, dead with their feet in the air, dead dangling over the boughs of trees. There was dead fallen three deep in creek beds and dead lying separately in a clearing tucked up to their chins in neat blankets of sun. I saw a head on its way to making a skull and thought about the belle and wondered if she was still wearing her own.

As we passed through them, we came upon many a crow still making itself a leathery meal. Most of what we passed had also been touched by the kind of carrion creatures liked to peck in pockets and sacks. See what treasures lay there hidden. We ourselves checked a sack or three as we went. There was miles still to walk and the pork and crackers had given out. One of the Akron boys said we shouldn't, leave the good dead lie and so forth, but I said whatever it was, they didn't need it anymore. Anyway, hadn't we already been crunching on the sandwiches of the dead? A quarter mile after I said this we found ourselves a sack shut tight had three good fistfuls of beef jerky wrapped in rose-embroidered napkins. There was a note had a rose motif at its top stuffed in there with the jerky. The note had got damp but some of it could still be ciphered. *Come on home, my darling son* was what could still be read. The darling son had on a blue, leaf-covered cap had come down cockeyed over his face. He had done his dying alone behind an alder bush.

It was getting dark when I figured we had notched the miles north we needed and began to true us west. It was poplars and creek bed for the next few miles and when we struck a village had lost its church spire to a cannon blast, our necks were cold and our feet were wet. There was a large group gathered next to torches on a kind of square. If they noticed us or cared about it when we came up out of the creek bed and joined them they gave no sign. There was a gal holding a dried flower sitting in a chair at the front of the crowd. She had her eyes closed.

'What is this?' I asked a smiling old grandpa leaning on a crutch.

'She's going to tell her story,' he said. 'Everyone wants to gets to sit and tell their story.'

'What'd he say?' said one of the Akron boys.

'Why are they telling their stories?' I asked.

'I told mine earlier,' the grandpa said. 'I told about my mother's pickled eggs. And her grasshopper soup. Back in Maryland. We had a famine. Come after the crops didn't make it. When I was young.'

'Why?'

'Shhh,' said a woman next to us. She was holding a baby didn't appear long for this dusky world. It looked like a hoarfrost had come down and done some of its designs on the baby's brow. Hurt to consider it. Baby had a head the size of an apple. Lacked only the worms.

'Because,' said the grandpa. He didn't say any more. Just

pointed over his shoulder at the woods we had walked out of. Then in the other direction at the church steeple wasn't there anymore.

'We're all going to be dead soon is what he means though he don't say it. That's the way of this war. You're going to kill us all,' said the woman holding the baby.

Then the woman in the chair started to speak.

'You all think I'm just Annie lives out behind the smithy comes and sweeps out your kitchens once in a while. Well, I'm not,' she said. She had a small voice. About the size of a popcorn kernel only got heated halfway at the bottom of the pot. But even the children in the crowd had gone quiet and there were only a few crickets and a kitten meowing some-where so her words came clear.

'You all think I am just the doorstep in the church and the bridge board on the creek, but I'm not.' She looked up when she said this. She wore a big smile, held it kind of slack-jawed. She looked from face to face in the crowd, nodding. One of the Akron boys leaned over to me while she was doing this.

'I think she's drunk. I think they all are,' he said.

'Shut up,' I said.

'I know how to walk where they aren't looking,' Annie said.

'What in hell does that mean?' the other Akron boy said.

'I know how to find the places where the world won't ever see me. I can walk in the shadow and I can walk in the light. You all want to try and watch me?'

There were nods from the crowd. The woman next to me

69

said, 'Uh-huh.' The grandpa gave a wave at the air with his crutch.

'You want to try and see me do it?' said Annie.

'Yes,' said the crowd.

'Well, I won't do it,' said Annie. 'It's just for me and never any of you mind. That's my story. And when the soldier boys come back to finish their job they won't see me even though I'll be standing right there.'

At this, Annie stood up and handed the flower to a man standing in the shadows beside her and he took her place in the chair.

'We got to get on,' I said.

'Stay and tell your story,' said the grandpa. 'Everyone gets a turn.'

'We got miles to walk.'

'Boy, those miles will wait on you. They won't go anywhere.'

'That's what I know.'

'I'll give you twenty dollars if you tell us your story. I got twenty dollars hid back of my shed. You can have it all if you'll tell your story.'

The grandpa had grown a kind of leer to him. He had his crutch up in the air again. There were others starting to look on.

'Tell us the story about how you are going to kill us all. Kill us and our babies,' said the woman holding her little apple-head thing.

'We don't want to hurt anyone,' I said.

'You won't hurt anyone,' the woman said. 'You can't hurt anyone. Not here. We're done hurting. Maybe we'll lay some hurt out on you.'

She said this and pointed up at the steeple had been obliterated, pointed just like the old grandpa had done, like it was the question had to be asked and the answer to the question both. As we walked away we heard the man holding the flower start up his story. He had a loud voice. Throat would have made a parade sergeant feel proud. His story sounded like a good one. Thomas Lord and his horse would have liked it. It was about long ago before the war finding a dead fish with a live snake in its mouth one week and a dead snake with a live fish in its mouth the next.

We hadn't got much beyond the squash-colored crackle of the torchlight when a woman wasn't any too young came swishing on up beside us and invited us all three to supper. We told her we had to get back to camp and she told us she had corn bread and fresh-slaughtered pig. I said no once more, but the Akron boys were already heading off with her. I called out I would leave them behind but they didn't listen and a minute later I saw my feet had betrayed me and I was following along. She lived a mile off the road we wanted on a rise looked out onto the valley we'd spent all that day trying to skirt. You could see the fires down there and hear the sound. The sound of an army settling down to sleep is a terrible thing. It is both loud and quiet. You can't like something that is both.

She had a neat little house the soldiers hadn't found when they'd come through.

'What kind of soldiers was it?' I asked her but she said she didn't know, that it had been dark, that she had been up in her house all alone.

'Must have been rebels, do you all manner of harm and call it God's work,' said one of the Akron boys.

'Sure enough,' the woman said in such a way you didn't know, not even to get started, what she was agreeing to.

I asked her her name. She said we didn't need names. That it was just supper. And a cup or two of something to keep us all warm. She said this then put on a pair of colored glasses. They had purple glass and had belonged to her late husband who had once played cards on a riverboat.

'He had a green eyeshade too but I can't find that. These help me see better when the lamps are lit. You ever try on a pair?' she asked. We all took turnabout putting them on then pulling them off. They made the room look muddy and had a funny shape to them. Hexagons. I had seen someone had sown a flower bed in the shape of a hexagon in town once before the war and told her this. She put the glasses back on and asked me what color the flowers had been. I told her, though I wasn't sure any longer, that they had been purple.

'What was your story?' said one of the Akron boys.

'I'm fixing to show you,' she said.

I didn't know what kind of hocus-pocus she and those glasses were going to get up to but she just led us out the back door, down a path, and into her garden. It was a fine patch. Well tended. Beans were good size. Eggplant and cherry tomatoes turning the moon to glow.

'You got a sleeping arrangement out in this garden,' said one of the Akron boys.

It was true. There was a bed sitting in the middle of the

green. It was a big affair, carved headboard, feather bed, pillows flounced in pink.

'I got a net I bring out against the mosquitoes. String a tarp when there's rain. You sleep in the garden, it's peaceful. The onions and lettuce get into your dreams. You can just go and go.'

We all four stood there and pondered this. There were crickets scraping around us. You get too many crickets around you and you feel like you're at the bottom of a bowl.

'You said something about supper,' I said.

She made no reply but after a minute more of cricket song we traipsed back into her house and she lit her lamps and pulled crocks of fresh cracklings out of her cupboard and a bottle out of a chest. It was a generous size of bottle and we all took our drinks from it. By and by we were as happy as a cackle of crows. Our hostess in her purple glasses was the happiest. She said when she had sat in the chair in town and told her tale they had all cheered. She asked the Akron boy sitting closest to her to tell his tale and when he had gotten about five words into it she stopped him and said, 'May I kiss you?'

He appeared struck. Took a hard swallow. 'If you got to,' he said.

So she leaned over and did the job. Right there at the table over cold pork and corn bread. She then asked if any of us could play the fiddle, that her old husband had left a fiddle behind him when he had gone off to 'feed his hopes to the slaughter,' and she hadn't heard a man's hands on it since that day. The boy hadn't been kissed got up then and took up the fiddle, turned it into tune, and started to play. This got our hostess and the kissed boy up to clabber arm in arm about the room. I leaned back and watched some of this but when the boy fiddling winked at me and started to play 'Gallant Ash' I got up, made my excuses, and walked out the door. A minute later I was back in the vegetables and sitting on the edge of the woman's garden bed. A minute after that I was lying down. I had on my mind that church steeple wasn't there and those graves in the forest that weren't graves. They were on my mind but I didn't know how to think about them so I shut my eyes. I drowsed some but got up quick when I saw the woman had joined me.

'Got those two all but asleep in there,' she said. She stood up after me and there followed a memorable farce around that bed in the moonlight. She would step toward me, her lips puckered, her arms up and good and set for a grope, and I would step backward and pivot away. In the moonlight her purple glasses glowed orange and rose. In between her attempts we would talk of the moon. Its ancient courses and seasons. She had read some poetry or her husband had and she made some remarks on it. Then she stepped at me again. This went on for a while. I got stung a time or two and wished we were doing our dance under a mosquito net. Presently she grew tired and we both went back inside. There wasn't much more to that night. Only that the Akron boys ended up finishing it just the two of them in that bed in the garden and I ended up with my head on that woman's table dreaming there was a boat leaving the world but I couldn't get on it because I was stuck to my chair.

We had six-inch-shell headaches and one of the Akron boys had caught a cough but we trotted off of the widow's property and away from that town the next morning like it had already been named target for cannon practice by the forces to come. We left off the trotting after a mile or two but kept up a good pace all that day and by and by the ragged boundary of our camp appeared. We didn't look any too smart straggling up the road but one of the pickets recognized me and waved us through. It was a Sunday and warm so there was more boys than ordinary milling in the woods and by the creek and in the big pond it fed into. The Akron boy wasn't coughing went off straight for the pond, pulling off his filthy clothes as he went, so it was just two of us continued along.

We passed a birch had nailed to it a big creeper toad. One of its legs was gone. It looked like a finger tap would crack it in two. We went by a maple next had nothing but ladies' names gouged into it. Jesamine, Turquoise, Apollonia, Marybeth, Ginestra, and so on. We hit the whiff of the camp just as we were passing the names and it didn't make them read so sweet. Fate of us all. Near the congregation of tents leaned a sutler's wagon looked picked over, but next to that wagon was a bench pushed up against a tree had a sign hanging from it said *Shaves.*

'Shave,' I said to the Akron boy still with me.

'Sure could use one,' he said.

This wasn't any more true for him than it was for me, for we were both as smoothbore as babies, but a shave was more by a bit than just a beard-scraping and we both of us fetched coins out of our pockets and sat down and it wasn't a minute later that we both of us had steamed rags drooping over our faces. After the rags had drooped the heat out of themselves the old brown fellow running the show pulled them off and made slow circles with fresh hot rags over our filthy faces and if I didn't gasp entirely out loud about how good it felt, the Akron boy did. When this part of it was finished the barber took still another hot rag and put it over my face and, after making a fuss with some shaving soap, went to work with his neat metal on the Akron boy. There wasn't any scrape sound to what he was doing, just a kind of quick, low swoosh, but that didn't stop him from tendering in some comments about how the young gentleman had sure been overdue and how he hoped 'all that hard beard' hadn't dulled his blade. When he had had his turn and it was mine, the Akron boy just slid right off the bench and lay down like dead Jesus on the ground.

'I've been born again to better things,' he said as he lay

there. Or he tried to say it. His cough had been holding off with the steam and soap but now it came back to him.

'We'll get you fixed up just right,' the barber said as he soaped my face. There was more lye in the soap than the kind I used when I had given Bartholomew his shaves in the kitchen at home but there was some lemon perfume to it too. *Swoosh, swoosh* went the steel through the soap. The instrument was old and had some rust on it but its edge was sharp. Every now and then as the barber swept my face, the owl-looking sutler owned the shop-and-shave outfit leaned out of his wagon and looked kind of mournful at us. I expect it was because his provisions had all been picked over and none too gently. Most of the times the sutlers made more money than Midas but there were other times that the boys got tired of handing over all they had for some stale moon cakes or stained sheets of paper and just took.

'How we coming?' I said when it seemed the pantomime had probably run its course.

The barber, who had been working with his face kind of close in to mine, leaned back a little like he was looking things over and said he just about had it, that there were still a few stubborn spots, but he was getting there.

I shut my eyes when he said this, but I did not drowse. Instead I conjured up the picture that I was at home in my own kitchen and that it was me holding the blade, me had stropped it sharp.

I had given Bartholomew a shave the day before I left for war. He hadn't wanted to talk to me much since that night in the yard when I had shoved him away, but that morning I got up early and milked his favorite heifer and picked strawberries and set them down in front of him before our work. If it wasn't the strawberries and cream set his jaw to working, it was the kiss I gave him on his ear, down on the hard part and onto the soft, and when I asked him if he wanted a shave into the bargain he took me up on the offer most courteously. He liked to sing while he shaved himself or I shaved him and that morning he sang happy songs had his foot tapping the floor so vigorous I had to tell him to quit or he might get cut. He quit his tapping but not his singing and next thing you knew he had found his way into a song had children in it, children running over hill and dale and couldn't find their way home. He sang at this awhile, getting quieter and quieter, and when I tried to kiss him again in the middle of it he wouldn't have my kiss, nor would he suffer my touch any longer, and stood with the soap still on his face and his beard half scraped, and when we worked that last day instead of standing shoulder to shoulder we did our working apart.

I talked to my mother inside and outside my head a great deal that day we worked apart.

'I am leaving here tomorrow and maybe forever, Mother,' I said to her.

*I know it,* she said back.

'I am leaving, Mother.'

80

*I know it.*
'I am leaving here.'
*Forever?*
'Isn't that what I said?'
*You said* maybe. *It's only forever if you don't come home.*

You think you are never going to get back and then you are there and you wonder if you were ever gone. The camp was still the camp. Beside the pond-bathing activities, there were boys fighting over hardtack biscuits and having wrestling contests in a leg-churned pool of mud. A mule got loose while I was walking by it, and I spent an hour at catching him with a gang of fellows had their shirts off against the afternoon sun. What a picture it would have made could I have joined in.

After the sun there was a cold rain and I discovered my corner of the tent had sprung a hole and spent some wet minutes in plugging it. During this storm a first lieutenant got caught with three helper women in his lean-to and was made to wear a barrel proclaiming the extent of his moral turpitude. Some of the boys who had robbed the sutler had been hung up under a beech tree by their thumbs. I barely got my eyes on either one of the Akron boys over those next days. You would have thought those tricks out in the woods hadn't happened. The lieutenant spent a fair portion of his time wearing that barrel with tears in his eyes. The boys had been hung up by their thumbs were let down. I started to write Bartholomew about what had happened in the woods and ended up describing that lieutenant, how he cried and cried for shame. I used another page to write down my thoughts about being back home in our kitchen, about giving him his shave, about how sorry for all of it I was.

Two days after I posted that letter I found myself again in the company of our Colonel. He had set up a desk in front of his tent to scribble out his letters and it took him a minute after I'd been announced for him to look up. He showed a little grander and grayer since our morning in the woods, but that must have just been the grand and gray of the afternoon settling down upon him. The weather will do all kinds of things to a man. It will make him look like a burned cinder or a pillar of ice or a pile of tapioca pudding left too long in the sun.

'Gallant Ash,' the Colonel said, looking up at last. I had expected the travails of the war would have chased that sobriquet out of his mind but there as elsewhere I was wrong.

'I have two things to discuss with you,' he said. 'But first I want to ask you a question. Would that be all right?'

'Yes, sir,' I said. For what else would you say to your Colonel?

'Have you ever met a man who was afraid to step out of doors?'

'Depends on if stepping out of doors meant getting fired upon, sir,' I said. 'Or getting cavalry-charged. I have stood fairly regular on the line next to men afraid of stepping out of doors and getting cavalry-charged.'

The Colonel looked at me nice and long.

'Are you afraid of stepping out of doors under such circumstances, Gallant Ash?'

'I would be a liar if I said I wasn't.'

'But you do it.'

'Every day I have to. Just like all your men.'

'Not all my men.'

'Most, sir.'

'Fair enough, Gallant Ash. Let's call it most. Most isn't bad. Most is always about the best we can hope for.'

'So we aren't talking here about de facto all your men.'

He laughed and I wondered if we had had our discussion now or hadn't. I did not like the way I was feeling standing there, and apparently we had not.

'I have a man in my company can't stand it to step outside. Has a good address in Yellow Springs, Ohio, and hadn't left it in five years before he took up the call to arms. Not even to sniff at the spring air. I know the village of Yellow Springs and the spring air there is fine. This man didn't want it even if it came in through the filter of his curtain. Claimed it burned him. Now he stands alongside you on the lines. I have watched him in battle and he does not flinch nor will he follow his fellows and hide behind fence or rock or tree.'

'Why won't he?'

'Because it is not bullets he is afraid of. He is afraid of the sun, the earth, the air, the all of it, the sky.'

'I don't know the man.'

'He is a close relation. My cousin.'

'In the infantry?'

'He refused a commission.'

'Why did he sign up at all?'

'Why did you, Gallant Ash?'

'Sir?'

'We have already discussed the loyalty of your heart and it is not a question that requires answering. I have had my eye on you since your tree-climbing exploit. I have seen how you can make a squirrel hurt. I am also aware of your recent adventure. I don't know and don't want to know how you got taken in the first place. I can chalk that up to rebel wiles. Were they wily, the outlaw rebel fucks who took you unawares, Gallant Ash?'

I did not answer his question. Just stared straight over his shoulder at the cot he had in his tent.

'All right,' he said. 'I'd not answer that either. Especially not as it included a vulgarity I lately find myself admitting too frequently into my discourse. Today I pose questions that deepen silence, rather than conclude it. That is the province of literature, not leadership. Aurelius knew this. I've just had Long's new version lent to me. Long is no fool. His *Aurelius* will serve our warring times. "Do wrong to thyself, do wrong to thyself, my soul." '

The Colonel turned and took up a book had been lying at

the foot of his cot. He opened it up to a page marked with a strip of purple leather and read to me. You ask me how I remember it these years later. I do not know.

'How quickly all things disappear, in the universe the bodies themselves, but in time the remembrance of them; what is the nature of all sensible things, and particularly those which attract with the bait of pleasure or terrify by pain, or are noised abroad by vapoury fame.'

The Colonel nodded and set the book back on his bed. 'My interest,' he said, turning to me, 'lies not in your motivation for service, for service is its own great answer, but rather in how neatly you extricated yourself and your fellows from that mess.'

'It was all three of us got out together.'

'Your gallantry exceeds you. I have seen and spoken to those two men. They are greenhorns and barely out of the nursery and I exercise the hyperbolic arts in referring to them as men. They would both be better as bootblacks. It is a shame of our days and all days of war that we set our children to arms. One of them cried as he spoke to me.'

'Like the lieutenant.'

'Pardon me?'

'He cried. In his barrel.'

'He has been demoted and sent to fight on elsewhere. Carousing was not his central transgression.'

'I didn't do anything special, sir.'

'All right.'

'It was three of us got in and three of us got out.'

'Fine, fine.'

The Colonel lit a cigar. He put it in his mouth and took it back out. The smoke came over to me and set a cloud between us.

'I'd had it in mind after your performance with those squirrels to make you a sharpshooter,' he said.

'I wouldn't want to be a sharpshooter,' I said.

'No, perhaps not, but I'd had it in mind for having seen you in battle and taken account of your exploits and having seen how you barely even had to aim when you shot those tree rats out of their skins. I'd had it in mind to recommend you, in addition, for a citation. For bravery. For that episode with the cartridge boxes. I know about that too. But you hear the tense I am using. You hear that I am speaking in the past.'

'Yes, sir.'

'There are other stories making the rounds about you.'

I took in a little suck of air. The Colonel's smoke came in when I did that, caught the wrong part of my throat, and I coughed. I saw the lady crossing through the moonlight behind the house. I saw and felt her both.

'Sir, I have been a good soldier and have fought well for the cause,' I said.

'A good soldier, is it? Is that the phrase your mind makes?

Is that what rises out of the mystery living its swamp-lit life between your ears?'

I took another breath. *I am coming home to you now, Bartholomew,* I thought. *Would it be such a bad thing? I should never have left and now I am coming home.* The Colonel stood. He was half a head taller than me. He had broad shoulders, and the gilt on his saber handle gleamed in the gray light. I felt small, and tired. I didn't know what I would wear. I had a sudden, wild wish that the stout lady's dress hadn't burned, that I had stuffed it in my pack and carried it back here with me.

'I had a man in here late this morning says you stole rations out of his haversack while he was at his nap.'

It took me a minute to hear what he had just said. When I had heard it, it took me another minute to take my mind away from the moonlight and that rustling sound I had made when I walked in the stout lady's fine cloth to the coarse blue wool I now had on my legs and the Colonel standing behind his cigar smoke in front of me.

'That man presented three others who were willing to testify that you had taken your fill of their rations too.'

'It is lies,' I said. 'I'll fight any man says otherwise. I will feed him my fists and ask him afterward how he liked his meal.'

The Colonel looked at me. He nodded.

'Maybe so. Maybe it is lies. Probably it is. I'd expect we could rouse just as many or more to refute the charges. Maybe

I don't give a good goddamn. But I imagine you can see that I can't offer you a special position or a commendation with such propositions swirling, can I?'

'No, sir.'

'I could not hold you to the light of general recognition and visibility under such circumstances. I couldn't put all eyes in this camp on you. You might find you couldn't move free any longer, that you had found your way into your own barrel, and then what would you do? Do you, Private, disagree?'

I shook my head. He nodded. He picked up his book again but did not open it. He closed his eyes.

''Of human life the time is a point, and the substance is in a flux, and the perception dull, and the composition of the whole body subject to putrefaction, and the soul a whirl, and fortune hard to divine.''

He tapped the book, opened his eyes.

''And fortune hard to divine,'' he said again.

'Yes, sir,' I said.

We stood awhile. There was some cannon pop off at a distance and some birdsong closer by.

'You may go now, Gallant Ash,' he said.

He looked at me and raised his eyebrow and when he had let his eyebrow down I went.

I am worn down to the bone,' I wrote my husband the evening after this exchange.

'Come home to me when you are ready,' he wrote me back. 'We can try again.'

'I am not ready, not yet,' I wrote.

'I'll keep on waiting, I will,' he wrote.

Then the Colonel gave orders and we marched across a strip of pretty water, over a low green mountain, and into the start of my hell.

# TWO

The battle lasted days. In our minds those days were weeks. In our dreams – taken in short heaps on the hard ground – those weeks were years. My company had been given a battery to help guard and some nights we had our rest under the cannon. The rebels kept us hot and more than once it was blade work under the stars. In the middle of a fight we got the order to drop and our boys fired off that six-inch right over our heads. The rebels had heard the order too and they dropped along with us so the only thing got hurt was an oak tree.

During the day they worked their mortars on us. You would have thought it was snowing dirt and fine flaked metal after a while. They killed a number of my company off for good but never took our cannon while we were at the guard. One time they tried a charge. To this day I will raise my weapon on any rebel I see, but the sight of a line of those fine horsemen coming at you through the smoke was a beautiful thing to behold. There was the part of the South worth keeping in that charge. It wasn't the part kept chattel slaves to scratch their masters' backs and make their beds. To work their fields. To build their houses. To whip when they wanted to. It was those horsemen, riding low, pistols at the ready, sabers up. They looked like knights. Like it wasn't powder black on their faces they were wearing but grim ladies' scarves on their sleeves.

We made our line and cut them down with our muskets and I saw our cannon take off half a handsome white gelding's head. They did not stop though and got close enough for swords and hooves and pistol work. You ever try to fight a man on a horse? Man with a weapon in his hand? Man come up from Natchez with the demon horse he was born on and hungry for blood? A boy not five feet away from me got made into jelly by a piebald mare with red eyes. Another got his head cracked right open with a pistol butt. I took a saber point across my arm and might have met my glory but a ball come out of nowhere took my ravisher off to his own. It was reinforcements. Four hundred walking blues to fight the one hundred horsemen. Only the grays had infantry of their own. I got a first lieutenant died five minutes later to tie a shirt-sleeve tight around my wound. When it was snug, I loaded my musket and went back for more.

We brawled and we brawled and when there weren't enough of us left to guard the battery, they sent up more fresh troops and offered us flank work in the trees. We had not one of us slept even a snack wink in two days but they had us double-time it. I expect I was not the only one could not hear from the cannon fire, and we ran to that fight in the woods in a silence I would trade the happy half of the world not to make the acquaintance of again.

I saw the Colonel in those trees. He rode up and made a short speech to his officers and then crossed his hands over his saddle pommel to wait with us. When he saw me, he said something. I couldn't tell what it was. He said it again and I pointed at my ears and shook my head. He nodded, lifted his chin, and looked a little ways down the line. There was a man sitting on a rock with his musket in his lap. We were all the rest of us dug in. I'd seen that man in a fight before. Stood next to him. I thought I could shoot quick but he was like a Gatling gun. I had a minute trying to picture his room in Yellow Springs with the air trying to get in the window to kill him. I drowsed into that picture and it took me far away. When I woke, the Colonel was still there on his horse and the man afraid of the whole wide world was still sitting on his rock, smiling about something and scratching at his knee.

Then all around us the branches went falling. The air next to my head tore itself open and let a ball pass through. One of my company lieutenants came and put his foot on the rock next to me, drew his pistol, and leaned forward. Someone shouted and I realized I could hear again.

'Hold steady, now,' growled the lieutenant.

Then like they had been there but invisible all along, you could see the rows and rows of gray and wore-out butternut starting to move through the trees.

It was five waves and by the fourth we were all down to but a few cartridges each. If it had been six we would have had to fight with bayonets and teeth. Somewhere in the fight, the Colonel had got down off his horse and stood along the line between me and his cousin. He had those big mustaches so you couldn't see his mouth but he had the look of a man had his jaw set. We'd been at it three good hours when I glanced over next to me and saw the two Akron boys. They each looked about ten years older. If they recognized me they didn't show it. They were dug in behind a dead tree about as deep as you could be but they were getting off their rounds. One of them died when the rebels tried a charge. The other one got swept away.

I saw the Colonel and his cousin until the end of it, though. The Colonel had rallied his officers to reform the line and now we lay waiting with hardly a bullet left for that fifth wave and not a cartridge box hadn't been pulled off the dead by me and many another left to sweeten our supply. The Colonel was standing next to his cousin, who had found his way back to sit on his rock. They both of them were black as chimney sweeps from powder burn and had cigars in their mouths. My lieutenant had been shot in the shoulder but he came up again and put his leg where he had planted it the first time.

'How we coming, Gallant Ash?' he asked.

'Drawing breath, Lieutenant,' I said.

'Well, draw you up some more and raise up that firearm,' he said. 'For here they goddamn come.'

They came and it was like a hot wind came with them and the air on either side of my ears began to burn and the world turned up and over. I was charging one minute and running back another. A boy twice my size kicked me in the stomach with his foot and I fell down into some fool's hole. Next thing I knew there was another in the hole with me and I tried to get my weapon around but saw it was the Colonel's cousin come down off his rock. He looked at me and he smiled, and well there might have been a rain of hellfire and the battle all around us, I can tell you right now he was the handsomest man I ever saw. It wasn't a handsome you could see down the line and sitting up high on a rock, it was a handsome you could see only up close, with death come a-calling, a handsome of soft cheeks and powder black and eyes set aglow.

'You're the Colonel's cousin,' I said.

'Did he acknowledge a relation?' he said.

The voice was as high and as handsome as the face. A voice scooped straight up out of a butter churn set to cool in a clear spring. He said a thing or two more with that voice but I couldn't hear him for the popping of weapons up above. A hot gust of wind came down into our hole and lifted his wet hair off his forehead and he leaned up close to me.

'I know what you are,' he said.

'I am a soldier in the Union army,' I said.

'I know that too,' he said.

'We got to get up out of here.'

I said this but I didn't move a muscle and he lifted his soft hand and held it to my cheek. He held it there and I did not move nor breathe nor shiver, only closed my eyes and let my face sit still against his hand.

When I opened my eyes I saw he had jumped up out of that hole and guessed he had run off to regain his rock. I saw him there when my cheek had left off burning and I had climbed out of the hole myself. He was standing on his rock and had his weapon raised. I had it in my mind to run over and get him to put his hand back up onto my face but my lieutenant came up beside me again.

'How we coming, Gallant Ash?' he asked me, just like he hadn't asked it a few minutes before.

'Drawing breath, Lieutenant,' I said, just like I hadn't said it either.

'Well, draw a little more.'

He said that and I heard the rebel cannon and saw the tree coming down at me and felt myself falling backward all at the same time. It wasn't at the same time, only felt like it was, because the lieutenant wasn't there anymore and the Colonel's handsome cousin was gone from his rock and the rebels were almost on us. A soft branch shoved me down then the trunk pinned me tight. I must have lost some of that breath I'd been drawing and taken a whack to the head because it seemed when I looked up through the leaves and branches that the grays and blues were taking turnabout in leaping over the rubbage above me, that the whole contest of the war was to be decided by who could most neatly vault the debris.

I slept then. Went wandering in realms of black and green. When I woke it was the deep hours. Stars lit the sky, bright burny things. Bigger than the springtime stars of Indiana. I started to count them but there were too many oak leaves in front of my face. I tried to clear the leaves away but found my arms were pinned at my sides. I could turn my neck and wiggle my toes and hands but otherwise could not budge. The breeze blew vigorous through my leaves for a good bunch of my breaths, and then it died. I heard more in its silence than I liked and shut my eyes.

I had walked out more than once of an after-battle and so had a fair idea of what lay clawing at the air that night around me. Ghosts of the new dead laughing down at what lay cut and burned and broken and still awake to it on the ground. Ours and theirs both had fallen and it was impossible to know what color cloth it was giving up those moans. One boy called out for his aunt Jane. Another was trying to whistle. Three or four wanted something wet to put down their throats. I expect every one of us there of either color had thought about those fights, like the Wilderness to come, when the wounded had been left where they lay and the forest had caught fire and gathered them all up in its burning arms. You would want a weapon if the fire was coming and you couldn't run. Something that would take you away on out of it quick. I could see my musket if I turned my neck as far as it would turn to the right. But even if I had been able to move I could see it was pinned down just about as neat as me. I caught the panic then. I shook and pushed and coughed and wriggled. Nothing. I had the trunk on my chest and arms and a branch across my legs. The tree wasn't much more than a sapling but it was tall and full of sap and had me good.

'I can't move because I got a ball in my back,' a voice behind me said.

'You one of us or one of them?' I said. I craned my neck around to the left and saw the bottom of a boot had a hole worn straight through it. It wiggled a little when I looked.

'I expect so,' the voice said.

'I'm just pinned down here,' I said. 'I'm not hurt.'

'Won't make much difference if you stay stuck.'

I didn't have any answer to this. Writhed at it little. Got nowhere. After a minute or two, of watching me I imagine, he spoke again.

'Looks like you got a scratch on your arm.'

I had forgotten about my arm. I had been aware of a pain but had not yet thought to verify it. As soon as he said this I felt it like some of that fire we didn't want to come had already set in to burn.

'That's about all it is, a scratch,' I said.

'I'd sure like a sip of water,' he said.

'Well, hold you on a minute and I'll run fetch you some.'

We both of us laughed at this, only his laugh didn't gallop on too long. You could hear it in his voice and in his breaths that he wouldn't keep creaking on much more.

'Where you from?' I said.

'That ground under you looks soft,' he said. 'Looks like it ain't much more than bits of bark and would succumb to some scratching. Can you move your hands?'

I moved my hands, pushed my fingers down. The dirt was as soft as he'd said.

'Where you from?' I said, moving my fingers, cupping and clenching.

'Work in toward yourself, carve out a cave, take it slow so you don't cramp, see if you can make a space.'

It had been quiet a minute but there was an unsubtle owl flew over the field and the moaning around us set up again. Someone called out to God to come down and kill him. To hit down on him with His great and thunderous hands. They would be spangled about every which way, those weepers and moaners. Just like they had been dropped off God's clouds. Away off in the far distance you could hear cannon fire. Big guns getting ready for another day. Make more happy glades like this one. There were foul smells drifting. Bodies couldn't tend to their business. Things opened up shouldn't ever have been.

'You know what I would like more than that sip of water,

more than just about anything besides this ball out of my back?' said the voice.

I was digging and making progress and did not respond.

'A fine, clean morsel of foolscap. Some fresh cotton rag. A creamy linen weave.'

'That ball has climbed up to your brain,' I said.

'I worked in a law office, down Carpenter's Lane in Richmond. I worked at copying on fine paper all the day long.'

'You're a Secesh.'

'Just a piece of paper. One sweet sheet. I haven't held anything but old scrap in a year. Wrote my letters home on a pile of old wallpaper squares. You ever try to write a nice hand on wallpaper? Paper's what you robbed us of worse than our homes and our lands.'

'I'm getting somewhere here.'

'I've got grandbabies. More than half a dozen. All of them live close. I was just teaching the oldest boy to write before I left. He knows how to hold the pen, yes, sir, he does.'

He gave out a cough, then went quiet. The fire in my arm felt like it was working down to the bone. It was my right hand did the bigger portion of the work. It was my right hand that carved most of the cave, that got me free. It was near dawn when I struggled loose. I lay there free for a nice long while then took the bayonet off my musket and stepped over to the reb. He was an old man with a white beard and had small, soft eyes. Too old to be a soldier. He looked too old to be anything.

My haversack was still around my neck. The first thing my fingers found in it was an apple. I ate that then reached them back in. Down at the bottom, folded neat, I found a sheet of paper. I didn't know if it was special but I had bought it recent to send to Bartholomew and apart from a few stray smudge spots it was clean. I unfolded it, took out my pencil stub, and wrote *Carpenter's Lane, Richmond,* then I folded the page back up and tucked it a little ways into his shirt.

My idea was to trot right off after my regiment but that's not how it went. I left behind my captor tree and found the way I wanted obscured. The dead and the about-dead lay left and right, forward and back. You had to pick your path careful. There wasn't light enough to see a clear road. I stepped on a leg and what was left of what it was attached to gave a shiver whose image when it rippled over the face I'd pay good cash money to have pulled from my head. One or two as could still open their eyes asked me for water. I was just about parched to the point that if they had had a drop of water on them I would have stole it for myself. I wandered this way and that, stumbling as I went. Now and again I would hear a cannon and think to march in its direction but the woods and slopes were cunning and played me clever tricks.

The light came on and I paused to gain my bearings. I do not know if I had been scrabbling for an hour or ten minutes, but just a corncob's throw over yonder sat the dead Richmond soldier and my captor tree. The boys hadn't been dead before had gone quiet. I hoped it was sleep of one variety or another. My arm had left off burning for the minute and was growing cold. I sat to have a look-see but fainted flat out when I tried

104

to pull up my shirtsleeve. I woke with the sun's fist in my face and a ringing in my ears. I rose and clambered up a slope and climbed a fence where a boy lay skewered with a piece of his face hanging down like a dewlap in the sun.

All the field ahead was filled with the dead. The local company of vultures had already crept through and turned out their pockets and carried off their canteens. Here and there you met a body part had broken off acquaintance with its owner. A glove had gone with a hand and a boot with a foot. At the middle was a dead bovine. I was not yet hungry and still had an apple and a cracker in my haversack, or I might have inquired after its meat. At the end of the field was another fence and another field. This field was empty of all but cannonballs. You could see where they had cracked through the trees and the paths they had made as they rolled. In the next field there was nothing but some ugly-looking thistles and the beginnings of a breeze.

Midday I came to a fine old manor house had been about burned to the ground. All that was left was the little gum-tack houses built all around it, mushrooms around a black rose. I poked my head into one or two of them and saw a cross and a magazine illustration of President Abraham Lincoln but nothing else. I looked down the well and saw what had become of the mansion's dog. It was floating on its side. The air smelled like smoke and the great swaths of mint sprouting deep green along the fencerows. At home Bartholomew and I liked nothing better than to take the scythe to a patch of mint. Two or three strokes and you had heaven climbing up your nose. Bartholomew could make a mint tea to beat the band. He would make it in the morning, set it in the root cellar, and we would drink it to cool off in the evening. Thoughts of the treasures in our cellar away up in Indiana got me to climbing down into the damp black ruin. Everything in the mansion cellar, though, had been hauled off or broken. There was blue and brown mason-jar glass everywhere to decorate the dirt floor.

While I was hunting down there for anything might have been missed I heard voices in the yard. I peeped out and saw it was a party of rebels, six strong. I crunched my way soft as I could back down and into a corner and waited with my musket. They didn't come down to the cellar, though. They were each one of them barefoot, and I expect they had tried their luck down amidst the broken glass before. As they were leaving I heard one of them say something about cooling off at a creek. You would think I would have lit out after them soon as they had left to get my own drink but instead what I did down there in the dark and the cool was breathe in some of the burned smell and think about mint and fall into a snore.

When I woke it was dark. I clambered up out of the ruins and went off in the direction I thought I had heard them take. My arm felt like an icicle, and my forehead was hot. There was a minute I saw my mother walking beside me and asked her to go away and get Bartholomew for me but she said Bartholomew preferred not to come. She went away and

Bartholomew did not come. When he did not come I got it into my head I needed to cry. Tears came up their tunnels but could not cut their way through the banks of dirt dried to my face.

On the outskirts of the farm was a clearing bordered by hedges gone wild and in the middle of the clearing was an urn. It looked pretty to me in the moonlight and I got the idea I had to leave something in it. Some token. A tithe. What you would lay down in the little basket at church. Good Christian passing by. I pulled up a fistful or two of grass and carried it over careful, like I was clutching a child. When I got to the urn and looked close I saw that others before me had had my same thought. There was a spoon in it and a broken plate and a tin pan that had done duty as a spittoon. I said before I can't sing but I sang and hummed a little as I dropped the grass back onto its ground and walked away.

I walked then down a tunnel made out of walls overhung by heavy fern. I went through a high gate led nowhere and bordered by strangled trees that twisted and yawed. I climbed a hill and saw line after line of ridges leading away into moonlit clouds. There was a hickory tree had had its arms cut off that I took it in my head to try to climb. I told it if it had had a young lady perched on its peak I would have made it to the top. For a time I followed an old road lined by trees. The road looked like it had once gone from someplace fine to someplace fine else and also that those days were gone. There were dead men sprinkled all around. You would have thought to look at them that they had just got winded and decided to plunk down. Have a smoke. Think it through a spell. One of these men wasn't a man. She had on a gray cap and was clutching a flintlock pistol had likely seen service in the Revolutionary War. Some of her chest wrappings had come loose and were dangling out of a hole in her shirt. You could see there was dried blood on them. She had been better built even just on army rations than I had ever been and I couldn't understand how she had hidden herself. I had an idea about sitting down and seeing if she could still palaver, that she might know some secret apart from masquerade devices could get me out of my mess. So I did a crouch-down in front of her but she did not budge. Every now and then as I walked on I thought I heard cannon fire but it was far away if it was anything and I could not be sure.

By and by, I came down a slope through trees wearing blankets of ivy and found the creek. I drank then. I drank, then retched, then drank some more and lay panting on my side. Then I pulled off my rags and unwrapped myself and took out Bartholomew's likeness, which was just a piece of hard metal in the dark, and set it next to me on the bank. 'We need to discuss our situation,' I said to the hard metal but the hard metal wouldn't talk, not any more than my dead sister soldier. Only my mother would talk to me. Only my mother could I count on. That thought, once I'd run it through my head, made me laugh out loud, and I sat there laughing like that until the mosquitoes found me, then I lay down on my side again and rolled over into the water. It was waist-deep quick and I played at sinking and rising. I got the idea then I'd been revived and set to work at scrubbing at myself with gravel and water grass. I scrubbed and scrubbed, then pulled my rags into the water and punched and squeezed them to dislodge the dirt. It was all of it slow work because I couldn't use my left arm. There were boys back in camp had used sticks to scrape off their extremities when they couldn't scare up soap and I gave that a try when I saw there were still streaks on my legs. I hadn't had a wash of any kind in three weeks. It didn't bother me a speck that I laughed as I worked. Or that I couldn't stop shivering even though I felt hot. After I had laid out my clothes I spent an hour or three crouched and gibbering under the bushes like I'd turned Akron boy and there were women murdering men around me in the dark. Then I stood and walked up the draw a ways to a spot where the creek deepened and spread. The rebel party were there, all as naked as I was.

'Gallant Ash,' they said. 'We heard all about you and your exploits. Come on in here and splash.'

An invitation as nicely put as that couldn't be declined. It transpired I'd saved that old Richmond man from certain death by giving him my piece of paper and he shed his grays like the others and came down with us to the water. I'd never felt happier since I had set out to war. Someone had a fiddle. Could give it a scratch. We linked up arms in the cool water and turned circles and laughed and frolicked about. I don't know what it was made the party take its turn but take a turn it did, and I found I had my good hand around a rebel boy's throat. All the others had gone, the old Richmond man included. It was just me and that rebel boy, just my hand and his throat. I killed him there in the water and let his dead body float away, then went back to my clothes. They were still soaked so I draped them over me and slept. In the dream I turned to next, my mother came to me. It was the old dream only now I had my musket. The angry crowd around me had lit its torches and grown tall so I laid about me with my bayonet.

I was sick and far from the creek when I opened my eyes. I had put on my wrap and clothes and found my way into the remains of a shelter looked to have been built for pigs. Clouds had come up in the night and there was a drizzle splattering through a hole in the shelter roof. I had been bitten up considerably during my sleep and, sleeping, had scratched deep gouges in my face. I could not move my left arm at all. It had swollen up against my coat sleeve. I felt for Bartholomew's likeness under my wrappings and knew at once I had lost it and when I got up on my knees, my stomach, which had nothing much more in it than mud and creek water, emptied out. It took me a time, kneeling there, to be able to open up my eyes and lift my head. When I did I could see a straggled line of our wounded coming down a lane. After my rich visions of the night before, I wiped my eyes and shook my head but the line did not waver. I stood and scuttled across the field and, breathing hot and hard, fell in with them. It was not the sorriest bunch I had ever seen, but it was close. There was more than a few missing digits on their fingers. There were shirts and underdrawers wrapped around heads. One fellow had about two feet of beard was clutching a torn, bloody pillow to his chest and leaving wet feathers to fall to the ground. I pointed at my arm when the man closest to me looked over. He just shook his head and opened his mouth to show me that he had been relieved of his tongue.

The hospital was in a school in the center of a village. The village had changed into rubble and splinters, and the schoolhouse looked like an island afloat in an awful sea. Everywhere you looked there were hurt men. All the ache of this world and the one beyond. The idea was that we would walk up to the doctors and they would look at us and decide who needed the quickest help. Those that needed it would go straight into the schoolhouse. The others would go and sit in the yard and offer up the wisdom of their ill fortune to the wind. As we walked up, some of the men had been sitting there a time gave out calls. One I went by lifted a blanket up to show a dead soldier. The deceased had had his clothes burned off of him, and his skin bubbled black, yellow, and brown. The man giving the show didn't say anything, just let us look a minute then put the blanket back down. An older man up ahead had a bandage on his head and drool caterpillaring out of the corner of his mouth said he hoped we all liked saws. Didn't matter whether you had a toothache or were carrying half a cannonball in your gut, they would cut something off. This set a few of them had already been doctored up and were lying in the dirt with their bandaged stumps to chuckling.

Meantime, there were screams coming from the schoolhouse. We got up to its side and could see to the back where they were dropping what they cut right out an open window onto a pile. There was a contraband grandpa with a cart loading some of it up. It was slippery work and he dropped a piece or two as he went rattling on his way. Out in the field, where he was heading, the carrion birds were having a contest to see which of them could fly off with the biggest piece. I looked at them and got up this thought those crows and vultures needed whiskey and cigars. I might even have said this out loud. Anyway, someone nearby gave a laugh. Up ahead, they were making the boys take off their jackets, sometimes their pants and shirts. One boy that had an angry, swollen slice down his side stood there naked as the day he was born.

I asked the tongueless man next to me to hold my place in the line and pointed over at the trees beyond the yard surrounding the schoolhouse. He looked out to the vultures and nodded. Another next to him, whose injury I could not discern, said he would help hold my place, all day if need be, unless of course I was going off into the trees to die. I walked through more hurt men as I made my way but these did not call out at me.

The first time I ever laid eyes on Bartholomew was in the yard of a house used to stand one mile due east of my farm. He had come with some other boys to see if it was true that the house was haunted and I had come to deliver a basket of sweet corn. The family had moved into the house was Irish or German or Italian or some such but the folks around here called them gypsies. The husband was far away on the railroad and it was just the woman and her two babies. I had got to hold them both. They were good babies, fresh and fat. I saw the boys trying to peek into a window and put down my basket and chased them off. Bartholomew stood his ground a minute before he ran. I got right up to him and he smiled at me, then he took off like a shot. The woman came out to thank me right then or I would have stood there and watched Bartholomew run. He was barefoot and had a floppy brown hat on his head. He was about the strangest thing I had ever seen. The next day he found me out where I was working a barley row and handed me a fresh-picked red zinnia. I'd never had a flower put into my hand before and I expect I stood there struck dumb. After he had handed it to me he did a little bow I never got him to repeat and again broke off into his run.

I could not run after I had left the schoolhouse-hospital grounds and climbed a fence and gone into the trees. My arm felt like it weighed sixty pounds and was pressed out everywhere against my sleeve. About half my head felt hot and the other half cold. There was a stinging down my legs like nettles had gotten in my pants. I couldn't run but I thought about Bartholomew running, those years ago, when he had been a boy and I had been a girl. At our wedding three years to the day after he put that flower in my hand we had a basket of zinnias. Every color they come in, though mostly deep, heart-smoking red.

You can't ever know when the dead world will come to you. Only that it will. My mother liked to tell me that. She who liked to send me down to the neighbor woman with any extra food we had. She who one night not a month after Bartholomew had handed me that zinnia walked through a crowd that had gathered outside the woman's house with muskets and pitchforks and lit torches and went and stood with her arms crossed on that neighbor woman's front porch. She had left in the night while I was asleep but I heard her leaving and followed her through the dark. When I came out of the cornfield I could see her pushing through the crowd. Beautiful and fearsome. Like a scythe through summer grass.

All this I chewed on as I walked that wood. Southern

115

wood, fern and creeper. It was deeper and darker than I had thought on parting its curtain. I had this idea that they might send someone after me and kept looking over my shoulder, though who amongst that sick company and those over-worked doctors they could have dispatched, I do not know. I tried to send hard thoughts to my arm. I thought to it that sick as it was or it wasn't, I would just as soon it kept hanging where it was.

I had to stop and rest fairly frequent but after a time of walking I managed to traverse the woods. It was dusk now. I came out onto a road that led over a hill to a town. Down that road a group of people were walking and in that group was a nurse. They had none of them seen me so I stepped back into the trees and when they had passed on a ways I went out again after them. The nurse had on a dark blue cape and a white cap was covered in filth and grime. Everyone in the group had soiled hands. The men had the dirt up to their elbows. I imagined the nurse did too. They walked fast. I kept expecting one of them to turn and ask me my business so I fried up some story I'd tell about why I was walking alone on the road behind them but not a one of them did. Not a one of them even seemed to notice me as I walked into town, past a cob-bler, a dry-goods store, and a stable, and saw where the group broke up and the nurse had her home. There was a dead-end alley next to the cobbler's with some boxes piled at the end of it. I walked back there and down that alley and dropped myself behind the boxes. I thought I would sleep but I didn't.

I lay there a long while, eyes open, looking up past the walls to the sky, past the sky to the stars, past the stars to my death out there, past my death to the final dark. Then I heaved myself up and walked over to the nurse's house. It was a cottage with a garden might have been pretty if it had been kept up. There was lamp lit on the front porch. A mat worn down to its nubs.

Her name was Neva Thatcher and she had thick brown locks. She had blue eyes and high cheekbones and small fine fingers liked to work at the air. She could swat a fly dead before you had seen it land, but she was slow when she didn't have to be fast. She never, the time I knew her, spoke loudly or needed to step first through a door.

She had been born up in Maine and had moved south with her husband before the war. This husband had gone off in the first weeks after Fort Sumter to fight as an officer for the Confederacy and had never come home. She had a letter from him, dictated as he lay blinded and expiring at Bull Run, that asked her to bid farewell to the sun for him, to pay his fondest courtesies to the grass, to salute the pretty waving trees. When the Union had taken her town she had quickly set aside the burden of her angers and gone to work in their hospital. She did whatever she was asked. Mopped floors, washed saws, dropped cut limbs out the window. Many times she would just sit and hold the hands of dying men.

She knew how to dress wounds and keep them clean. She had first thing I arrived dressed and cleaned mine. She had let me lie down on her own bed and had kept the curtains closed and fed me soft bread and stewed peaches and dripped water from a clean rag into my mouth. When she had seen what I was, standing there on her front step and none too gently dying, she had said nothing, had just taken me by the arm that wasn't swollen and led me in.

I stayed three weeks in her little house and when I began to be well enough she gave me one of her dresses and helped me to a chair in the kitchen and let me sit by the open window and suck a little at the breeze. She had good rations of salt and sugar and sowbelly and hardtack and fresh bread for her work for the cause. She shared them all with me. She liked to read. Had a wall full of books. Each day she wrapped one or two of them in a cloth and carried them off to the hospital to read to the men. She read to them about hearts and flowers and pharaohs and mountaintops and clear-running brooks. She read to them about Jerusalem and chariots and trumpets and ghosts and lambs. I know what she read to them because in the evenings she would read to me.

Tired and whipped as I was, some of the gay finery of the images she was conjuring rubbed me wrong. I expected the Colonel wouldn't have thought anything too much of them either. But you couldn't hold it against her. She didn't seem to need any of it to mean too much. One voice saying soft things into another's ear. She was as wore out as any of us and every morning like any of us who was able she rose and did her work. She didn't give the day too much of her smile but she had one. I saw it. She had a china service was her pride and joy. Came from a grandaunt back in Maine. Flower and animal was the theme but about every piece to the service was painted different. Neva said it was the work of more than twenty hands. There were doves had an eager look to their eye peeping out from behind indigo roses. Yellow cats asleep under dogwood. Owls perched on plum trees. Wolves howling next to holly. Cows and sheep nibbling buttercups in a field. The service had lived through the trip down south and it had lived through the war. The teapot to it was Neva's greatest treasure. You did not have to work at it too hard to look over her shoulder as she dusted at it and admire the shades of pink seemed to have come off real roses, the careful greens seemed to have come off real leaves, the deep blues of the feathers of its many birds. The teapot was Limoges, she said. Her grandaunt had painted it herself and Neva gave it a swipe about every day I was with her. Each time she did that chore there would alight on her face a smile.

'For all it is made of so many different designs, this china service is my miracle of constancy,' she said one day I was watching her. 'There were soldiers in this house before I started to work for the hospital, every one of them ready to desecrate my sweet china. The captain with them who ordered it to stop before it had started knew my husband before the war. I served him tea out of this very pot.'

Still, many was the time after her long work she would come in, wash off her hands, see to my arm, then cry herself straight to sleep. She had kept canaries, a favored present from her husband, in a large white cage in the parlor, but whether she still had her grandaunt's china or she didn't, now the canaries and the husband were dead and buried and there were moments she could not bear even to hear a sparrow chirp.

She spoke of love and love brought to ruin by war. It did not trouble her to betray the cause her husband had fought and died for, she told me. The Confederate States had seceded out of stubbornness, and war had come and taken her husband away. She would move north when it was finished. Take her china and return to the village in Maine she had left all those years before.

'If they will have me,' she said.

'Why wouldn't anyone ever have you?' I said.

'This war,' she said. 'This war, this war.'

The flesh of my arm crept each day closer and closer together. Like two ragged companies didn't know yet they were fighting for the same side. When I saw I could comfortably rest my left forearm on the table again, and hold myself to purpose, I asked Neva for paper to write on. She that evening brought me home a fine fresh stack. It was hard to look at the linen cream of that paper bought nice and neat from one of our Union sutlers specialized in officer wares and not think about the old soldier from Richmond. I thought, too, as I sat there and looked at that paper, because how could you ever not, about all my battles, about my days in the camp, my walk through the woods with the Akron boys, my talks with the Colonel, the soft hand on my face come from his beautiful cousin, my time caught tight beneath the tree. I wrote Bartholomew that I had stepped out of my uniform and lost my musket and his likeness – for I had left it in the mud by the creek – and now wore a dress again. My legs felt free and some of the rest of me did too. I had hurt my arm and feared to lose it but here it was holding down the fine paper I was writing to him on. I sat and talked with another woman, I wrote him, and it was good and easy to do so. I thought of my mother and it did not trouble me. 'I feel I am sitting outside of it all and can breathe and look at it a minute and not choke on the dust in my mouth,' I wrote. I know I wrote this and that it was received. I have the letter sitting here beside me.

When I had finished writing, Neva brought me candle and sealing wax and, the next morning, carried my letter away with her. Sent it limping up to Indiana by the first post. The next morning after that, I tottered in from the garden to tell her my arm was no longer tight against my dress sleeve and found her in the kitchen wearing the rags of my uniform.

'Show me how you march,' she said.

'I don't remember how to march,' I said.

She pouted a minute, worked at slicing cheese and snapping crackers. Then she stopped that and came to me, slowly with the first steps, then quickly with the last, then slowly she kissed me. I let her do this for a time. Her mouth tasted like linden berries of all things and I realized I couldn't remember what Bartholomew's mouth tasted like. It occurred to me that my own mouth must taste a little like the late pansy flower I had just been chewing on. We stood both of us, Neva and I, with our arms hanging at our sides and only our mouths pressed together. There was a moth in the kitchen. I could see it with my left eye. It sat waiting for night's dark above the garden door. I moved my head a little to see it better, and Neva's eyes came open. When they did I put my hand on her arm and pressed her away gently to make her stop. She stopped. She kissed me again the next day, nice and quiet this time and not in my old uniform, and again I let her and again after a time I had her stop.

The day after that second time, she made stewed oysters and corn fritters dressed in maple syrup and served it to us on her good china plate. This was the plate had on it monkeys climbing cherry trees. I had seen a monkey in a cage once in town. These monkeys looked bigger. Like if they wanted to they could tear down the trees. As we ate at our oysters they seemed to move. They would leap a little higher up their tree when I was lifting my fork but each time I tried to catch them at it they again slipped down. When we had finished our supper, Neva poured hot water into her pot and made us chamomile tea. We held cups favored handsome with golden lilies and blood-dark laurel leaves. She took my hand for a time, then she let it go. We leaned back in our chairs and she asked me if I wanted to hear a story, and though I feared a little she might reach for one of her fair volumes I said that I did.

The tale she told, which did not come out of one of her

books, was about a cousin who had gone west from Maine to help shepherd some poor band of argonauts to California back in 1842. They had headed off west seeking gold from the ground or gold from the land or gold from the sea. Half Neva's whole hometown had caught the settling fever for a while but only this cousin had actually gone, and not for any gold he thought he could have for the easy pickings but for the considerable riding fee. He had left off alone one early morning and Neva had stood with those who waved and watched. They had not seen him again for years.

The argonauts, which was the term he had used, even though they were no Greek explorers, just men and women bent on making it west, had done well for a while, the cousin had told it those years later upon his return, and then they hadn't. The man had hired him rode off one day with some others to scout for water and didn't come back. He was left with the man's wife and two daughters. They had started out from Springfield, Illinois, with a hundred wagons in the train and little by little they worked it down to sixty-one. The train had split after the Wasatch, and the cousin had continued on with the woman and her daughters in a company much reduced.

When the Indians came it was in a fury and number that they hadn't had enough muskets by half to answer. The woman's two daughters were among those who were taken. The woman, said the cousin, had not waited even until dawn to set off after them. She had just grabbed a musket and walked

124

off in her yellow dress and bonnet. The further diminished train, now just four or five wagons, had regrouped as best it had been able and continued on. Three days later at dusk the woman had walked into their camp with her daughters and three other children in tow. When pressed, she would not say how she had freed the children, only that it wasn't any use to go after the others taken because they were all killed.

The argonauts made it to California and the woman and her daughters had gone to live with some of their people and that was the last the cousin had ever heard of them, though he had offered up that he hoped the woman had grown as rich as her courage. When Neva Thatcher had finished this story she brushed back a brown curl of hair, took a sip of her tea, and told me if I wanted she would give up on her project of going back home to Maine and that I could stay and live with her here. She had a wedge of land out in the country-side I could cultivate if I liked. It was bottomland, rich as rabbit stew. I did not answer, just sat still and looked at her, couldn't find any word I could say would correspond to the story she had told about the woman who had gone off into the wild to get back what had been taken from her and what she was asking me.

My world had shrunk those weeks to the size of Neva Thatcher's little house and yard, and leaving aside the question of kisses, I had gotten comfortable in that world, had found it fragrant, even cozy. Meanwhile, as I discovered when one morning we went out for a walk, the town beyond her fences had been turned during my convalescence into a privy, and the land around the town into a rubbage ground. Union army wagons with broken axles lay in the fields like the bones of lost things had once bellowed and breathed, and everywhere you could see broken munitions of various descriptions and snapped bridles and rucksacks cut or torn. There was a boot-ruined field on the edge of one of the camps and on the hill beside it was an abandoned gallows. We crossed a brown skull or two, one of which had a broken cavalry sword stuck through its eye. I saw something shiny at the edge of a reedy pond and pulled out a bugle had been given an extra twist. We passed a old slave-selling emporium had had its main sign pulled down and its front door, frame and all, stove in, no doubt to facilitate, Neva told me, the egress of all the ghosts had still been whistling around inside it.

'I take it you are against the institution,' I said then.

'Honey, there are plenty of us down here, imports or otherwise, who never held with it.' She spit as she said this. The gob landed near my foot and she begged my pardon. She touched my hand with two of her fingers when she did. 'They used to stand them over there,' she said, pointing at a wide piece of wood plank outside the emporium. 'There was one time it was just boys and girls, each one of them wearing one of those masks. You could see about all of them, young as they were, had been whipped.'

'Did they get sold?'

'They always got sold.

'My husband,' she added, after we had put our backs to that place, 'fought for the Confederacy but felt much the same way.'

Soldiers walked hither and thither in company or alone and a number of them called out to us on our walks. If they had dark soldier thoughts, though, they kept them to themselves and mostly they paid us courtesies and called out to Neva Thatcher by name. We walked farther each day away from the town, and the garbage and soldiers trailed off and by and by it was just the stripped and battle-burned land. I'm painting up a picture of a world gone off to its glory and never coming back and woe to us all, but with every minute my lungs worked on those walks, my head felt lighter and my mind felt clearer and a kind of giddiness galloped up and overtook me. I gave out a happy laugh then when Neva Thatcher took me over a hill and showed me a corner of the hundred and twenty acres had been her husband's and said once more if I wanted to I could stay and work it after the soldiers had gone. I still didn't answer but laughed again and even turned a frolic or two as we walked down a few of that hundred and twenty acres' ruined rows. For a minute some fat sow hadn't been shot and cooked came out and gave a snuffle into the field and I told Neva Thatcher I was going over to see if I was strong enough to pick it up.

'I used to be able to pick up a good-size pig,' I said and saw in my mind that first pig my companion and I had shot near that shed full of chain in Kentucky.

'Stay here and be my friend and farmer,' Neva Thatcher said, putting her hand on my arm as I thought these thoughts.

But I had grown quiet for thinking of Kentucky and its pigs and wasn't much company to Neva then or after we returned from our walk. Back at the house over a bowl of corn soup I cheered up some and offered up an apology, to which Neva answered that I must never, but for the gravest offenses, say that I was sorry. We took walks after her work the rest of the days I was there. On one of those walks I hitched up my skirts and gave a try to see if I still remembered how to run.

'You trot admirably, I'll give you that,' called Neva Thatcher from the other end of the stretch I'd sprinted down, 'but now take a look at this.'

I have seen a handsome number of years since then, but I have never beheld anyone, not even Bartholomew at his best, run as strong and speedy as Neva Thatcher did that day when she hitched up her skirts and came running in my direction across the earth.

The days crept their cool ways past and Neva's kisses came closer together and the soldiers in the street gave signs of a great muster to be held and I knew it was time for me to leave.

'They would have taken my arm off; it was you saved me,' I told her my last night in her house. It was late and she had come like she came every evening now to kiss me.

'It was you your cousin was talking about,' I said. 'You were the one who walked into the wild and saved someone.'

'I have never been to California,' she said.

'Doesn't make the story any one word less about you,' I said.

'And here I thought it was about all of us.'

'Us?'

'Every last one.'

'I don't follow you.'

'You are better, aren't you,' she said.

'You made me better. And I thank you for it.'

'This is a leaving speech.' Her voice dropped. 'I know one when I hear it.'

'I'd like to return to my regiment.'

130

'Won't they be far away by now? Perhaps even on the other side of the world?'

'I think I can find them.'

'Why not just go home? To your husband man. Go on home if you won't stay here. If you won't stay with me and love me a little and work my farm.'

I shook my head and she gave me up her smile and kissed me one last time in this life and when I woke there were four Union soldiers and an officer standing by the bed. Neva was leaning in the doorway behind them. She didn't speak when they hauled me up, just handed them my old uniform, watched them drop a rough-cloth dress over my head, and let them kick and cuff me and call me a spy and take me away. She came that evening to visit me in the cell they rigged out of the sheep shed and tossed me in down next to the stable.

'If you had just said you were going home to your Bartholomew and not back to the war instead of staying here with me. If only you had said that, I could have stood it,' she said.

'You let me out of here, I'll go back to him,' I said. 'Or how about I stay with you. You tell them to let me out of here and I'll stay with you and we can run races and pick up pigs every day.'

'You didn't pick up any pig and we already know who would win those races,' she said.

She had brought me two hard-boiled eggs and she helped me peel them. She looked me in the eyes the whole time I ate.

Then she went away. In the deep and dark hours of that night I thought she'd come back, for I woke out of a doze hadn't taken me any farther away than the backs of my own eyelids and saw a figure sitting near me. It shifted though, or the moon outside the window found a way to move, and I saw it wasn't Neva. It was another woman altogether, one the lay of the moonlight had lent a single golden eye.

'How did you get in here?' I asked.

She didn't answer. Just sat there. Kneeling, it looked like. Hands in her lap. My own hands were bound. She had on pants and a broadcloth coat. Below the eye I couldn't catch blinking you could see the long curve of her cheek.

'I was sleeping,' I said.

No answer. By and by the moonlight had lit her eye left it and in the darkness she stood.

'Keep a distance, now,' I said.

But she stepped forward and to my side with a movement geared quicker than I liked and after she had stood there awhile breathing cloudy breaths into the cold air, she leaned her head in close to mine. I wanted to turn my own head and look at her but found I couldn't.

'You come any closer I will fight you, even tied up as I am,' I said.

'Close your eyes,' she said.

It was my turn to stay silent. The voice was large but she was not. She wasn't any much taller than a child.

'I'm not closing my eyes,' I said at last. She lifted one of her hands up past my face and into the moonlight had found its way back into the stall. There was a knife in it. The knife climbed up through the moonlight and back down. It made this journey several times. When she pulled it away from the light and placed its edge against my forehead, I thought the gold air before me would start to bleed, and when she pressed the blade harder against my forehead I thought that in its bleeding we would both drown.

'Close your eyes now, Ash Thompson, killer of men, or I will cut out your tongue and feed it to the fishes,' she said.

I closed my eyes.

'You tell Neva I was already sorry,' I said.

'Who is Neva?' she said.

Came a scuffle of feet and a cough from outside the shed door. I felt the air in front of my face open and shut like a ball had moved through it. I kept my eyes closed for a long time. When I opened them again even the dark was gone.

They held me in that stall two days past that night. I tried to ask my guard about the girl had come to visit but he wouldn't answer me. Neither did he say anything about the red line he must have seen I had across my forehead. One of those days they had in another stall a pair of Confederate officers of one kind or the other who spent their time in singing duets about beautiful ladies and the bounty of the lands of the South but otherwise never said any other word. The last morning, my guard and four or five of his friends came and leaned their arms over the top of the stall and looked at me. Then they dragged me over to their camp to be hanged.

There had been word of a spy in the ranks, a whore from Chattanooga dressed up just like a man. This spy had passed on troop movements and gotten a barley field's worth of boys torn to bits. It was a first lieutenant told me this. Every now and again while he was talking he would pull his handgun out of its holster and point it at me. Once or twice he cocked the weapon. I counted two good teeth in his mouth. There were a few other junior officers present and a number of men from the ranks when he conversed up close with me.

I kept my composure through this, stood as tall as they

would let me, looked the broke-tooth lieutenant straight in the eye, told him I had had other interviewers to scare me, that he would have to work twice again as hard as he was if that was his aim. I told him that I was no spy, that I came from Indiana, honest farm country, land come down to me through my mother, that I had never been to Chattanooga, didn't even know what that was. I gave him the letter of my company, the number of my regiment. I listed the engagements and battles I had fought in. I told them to speak to the Colonel, that he would vouch for Gallant Ash. They laughed at this, said Gallant Ash was just a story some fool and his friends had told to pass away the days. The company I had spoken of was made out of Ohio men, not girls from Chattanooga or Indiana or anywhere else I claimed or didn't claim to come from. They were still laughing when a major pushed through the crowd and asked for an explanation. He and the lieutenant stepped off to the side.

'Is there no one here who remembers me?' I said. 'Look, I have a saber scar on my left arm.'

The men around me neither spoke nor moved. I must not have looked like much in my dress and trying to show my scar in the middle of all those men, because when the major came back over he walked straight up to me and took me gently by the elbow.

'If she is a spy, she will receive a trial,' he said. The men had been hunting blood and had not had it and were none the happier, but when the major spoke again they moved away.

He was very kind as we walked. He was tall and pleasant-looking and had a sweet voice. He told me he came from New York, the shores of Lake Erie. He told me he would write to my company commander and apologized for the conduct of his men. I told him I knew a thing or two about men brought to the brink and hard pushed, that I had stood alongside them many a time, that I could not hold the ugliness of war against them any more than I could against myself or those I had considered my friends.

'Why did you refer to yourself as Gallant Ash?' he asked.

I told him. I described climbing the tree and the looks of the men below. I described it at some length. I am not sure but what I might have given out a chuckle or two as I told the story. Might even have tapped a foot and sung. The major nodded. He released my elbow, which he had been holding so gently. Said he had heard a song about Gallant Ash and was pleased to have met the one who had inspired it. Kindness comes in many colors. He called me miss, thanked me for my service to the Union cause, and bade me farewell.

My Bartholomew never learned his way into or out of a fight but there was one thing no one could hold the candle to him at and that was dancing. If he even started to sniff the arrival of a song, he was jumping and kicking across the floor. In our earlier, happier times he would sing himself into a dance if there wasn't any other music for it. I expect I wasn't the worst you ever saw at dancing but I was a long way from having the gift. Another lifetime Bartholomew could have been up on the stage. That would have been the life for him. That voice of his could bubble up out of his throat and the way those arms and legs of his could move. Still, we only get but the one life and I never heard him calling out for any other. Except of course for when we first met and he called out for the life had me in it. He called loud to step into that. While he was courting me, is what I mean. I made it take a while but he got it done.

He said, 'I got nothing to offer but sweat and zinnias.'

He said, 'But I will love you until the day I die into my wings and know you have died into yours.'

He said, 'There won't ever be any other one loves you as true as the blue of this blue shoe.' He held up his shoe for me to look at when he said this. It was kind of blue. Kind of green too. Looked like he was wearing birds on his feet. And then he danced for me. He had rolled an old whiskey barrel all the way out from town and had set that barrel in the yard and had hollered for me to come out of my house and he hopped up on that barrel and danced like a dervish in a mulberry bush or a monkey had a toothache or a rhinoceros had a head-ache or some such and then he hopped back down and when he saw I'd started up breathing again he said what I've already told, then said he wanted to marry me.

'Why?' I said.

'It's love pure and simple,' he said.

The day Bartholomew and I got married we danced. There was a small group had gathered and they gave us a clap and a cheer and when it was done we walked out the two of us to the cemetery to see my mother. She had a stone wasn't much but I had kept it well enough and it had never wanted for flowers. We lay bluets and sweet peas down on it and stood a minute and then I said to Bartholomew, 'Now, that's done.' And he said, 'What is?'

I hadn't known just exactly what I meant when I said it but I knew some choice part of me hoped by turning a dance with my nimble-foot husband and then laying down those flowers on my wedding day I could let some of that which was past trot away. I told him this as we walked home and he was quiet a time and then said he expected it wouldn't work out that neat. Which wasn't the last time he was right. I went on thinking about my mother every day just as I had before I had gotten married only now Bartholomew was there and the smells and sounds of the past didn't scorch quite so hard, didn't make me stand and slash at the air with a stick or run out hunting more often than I had to. They were still there though, those smells and sounds and sights, and they chewed and worked at me like worms in their corridors, and then other worms came with their own mouths to chew and keep them company. After a time, like I've told it, I packed up my bag and went to war.

There are other memories now come to join the one of my mother standing on the neighbor's porch steps, the neighbor that left here with her babies long ago, and of my own baby, who died beside me not an hour into his own life on our plank-wood floor, other spells of the past that won't be put aside. One of them is of that place they took me after the kindly major made his bow and stepped away. The men he assigned to escort me took me back into the town and even past Neva Thatcher's little house so that I thought for a minute, forgetting how I had ended up walking the thoroughfares under guard in her dress, that they were going to let me go back to her. She could keep me on awhile, I thought. She could kiss me morning, noon, and night if she needed to. Then I could tell her, when she had got tired of that, I was going to go back to my Bartholomew.

We went straight on past the little house, though, and on down the street and along another and then they loaded me onto a wagon and took me away. Another town. It was night-fall when we got there and the building we stopped at was tall and wet-looking with windows on the top floor had narrow bars on them. It was made of gray boards had been dusted up with musket balls and you could see even in the light of the streetlamp that part of one wall had been blown open and rebuilt. I had tried to talk a little to the men guarding me but they had refused to speak except amongst themselves and said no word to me as they brought me down off the wagon and handed me over to another guard. This guard would not speak to me either. He took me down a hall had straw and things that crunched on its floor. We went past doors had moans and murmurings behind them. Came every few feet or so past the muffled clink or drag of some chain. At the end of the hall was a door and through that doorway I was pushed.

When I saw where they had taken me I did not turn and bang the boards and holler to be let out, just as I had not whimpered before when the lieutenant wanted to put me in the ground, nor run, not even once, when the guns had blazed on the field. There were eyes in that place they had put me. Like that girl from the sheep shed had found a way again to keep me company. They were all in a line along the sides of the room. They were every one of them looking at me.

'I was out of my head a little in the woods, but that was because of my wound,' I said aloud to the eyes. The only answer was a sound came from the corner. It was like bones boiling and cracking in a pot. *They every one of them have knives,* I thought. Then there was a laugh and the eyes all went shut. After I had stood a minute with my hands and back pressed against the door, my heart beating full hard enough to break the boards behind me, I let my legs lead me down to the floor.

It was a lunatic house from the old days. Had stood there holding tight its horrors many a year until it had had its sides opened by stray cannon shot in the early days of the war. The keepers had run away and the lunatics had poured out into the countryside. Some had found their way through the battle and never come back. One went off looking for the well he had been dropped down in Georgia during the first part of his treatment twenty years before. He didn't make it past a pond on the outskirts of town. There were two from the women's side of the house went with him. Mad as they were supposed to be, they pulled him out of the pond five times before the battle cooled down and some of the locals got the idea to hit him on the head and tie him to a tree. There had been a fire on the men's side and a number of the ones chained up had burned.

The fire had worn itself out and the hole in the wall had been patched and some of the lunatics had been rounded back up. The building had locks and chains aplenty so the army had taken to using it for anyone they thought had their firing pins loose. The men's side was full to bursting with boys had gotten addled up during the fight. Some they let back out. Some they didn't. I was in my room with two ladies had seen their children blown straight out of their skins in front of them and couldn't quit wringing their hands. They could talk well enough, just couldn't stop wringing their hands. There was another supposed spy, this one from New Orleans was the charge, who wouldn't say a word. There were a couple of gals had been locked in, as far as I could get out of them, for being too heavy. They both of them walked too fast when they came at you and weren't heavy anymore. The three or four others were the old customers. They wore chains most of the time. One of them liked to talk about the Gadarene that Jesus healed way back in the long ago. About the pigs He had put the Gadarene's demons into. About how the pigs had flung themselves off the nearby cliff. How the demons had had to find other homes. 'Other homes,' she liked to say with a smile shaped like a snapped-off spider leg could have curdled fresh milk, and she'd lift her chained arms to indicate all of us, those in the room and those without. Another of them liked to grind what teeth she had left. Did it awake or asleep, morning, noon, and every inch of the night. She got hit at considerably for it. Even I got grouchy a time or two when, just after I'd got my eyes shut, she offered up that sound.

Once a day one of the old keepers, big gal, would come in with some porridge for us. She came with kicks and cuffs too. I wasn't spared this courtesy. She had a soldier with her each time she came in or I might have tried to answer her. Every now and again some fellow as said he was a doctor would

143

peep his head in through the door. Just as soon as he had had that peep he pulled his head back out. We would a few of us yell out to him when he paid these visits but if he heard us he never gave any sign.

Sometimes several of them came into the room in the evening with buckets of cold water. We each got one of these over the head. It was a long night of shivering on the floor after they had gone. There was other things going on at the men's side. There was more than one that set to screaming regular over there. At first it sounded like it was all just one screamer. Then you heard them enough and knew it was several and got to know each individual one. You can scream high. You can scream low. You can scream something in between sounds like steam out of a train whistle. You can scream so it sounds like a musket bullet been sent by your ear. You can scream like a monkey. You can scream like an elephant oak struck by lightning in a silent wood. There was a boy across the way screamed like he was singing. Like they ought to sign him up for the stage. There was a curlicue elegance to his scream and I got to wishing it was just him they would poke at with their sharp sticks.

Once each week one of us with a guard at her back would carry out the slop bucket. I got detailed to it more than my ordinary share because I didn't faint or try to bite anyone when I was doing it. I kept moving forward. Step at a time. Even when a soldier tried to trip me up for some fun, I did not stop. He stuck his big foot out and I fell forward but caught

144

myself and the bucket both. Managed too not to hit him one
for his joke. Just smiled. Like I understood and even agreed
with what it was was making him laugh: lady about fell with
a bucketful of shit. The slops got carried to a trough in an
alcove let out to a stream at the back of the yard. When the
stream wasn't moving much, the heavy part of the slops
stayed put.

Carrying slops wasn't the only job they let me do. Once
when I was carrying a bucket I passed a soldier giving another
a shave. They were in the cold sunshine and the one was having it done got his face cut by the other and cried out.

'You're holding that blade wrong, for one thing,' I said to
the fellow playing at being a barber.

'How in fuck's he supposed to hold it?' said the fellow had
been cut.

I put down my bucket and came over and showed him how
it was done.

'You stink like a sewer, little sister,' said the one I'd taken
the blade from.

'He ain't wrong,' said the other, 'but you keep on.'

I shaved him, then shaved his friend, and every now and
then after that I got called on to scrape a face. Mostly it was
guards but twice or three times there was a prisoner in the
mix. These were big-bearded things attached to some flaps of
skin, some ruins of shoulders, some piles of bones. When I
shaved them up there wasn't anything left to them. You could
of just dug at the dirt and kicked them straight into the hole.

They were happy, though. Smiled and winked. Appeared these shaves were a kind of treat. Given out by the guards for good behavior. Maybe they were the ones didn't scream. Some of them had been soldiers couldn't stand the fight any longer. Boys that had run away from the bullets or been found back in camp having never left their bunks. One fellow I cleaned up had the wringing-hands problem. Didn't stop him from smiling like it was Christmas morning when I got the hair off his face.

It wasn't just jolly shaves in the yard for the men prisoners in that place, though. Coming and going from the yard you went by a chair set in a cell didn't have any door. Sometimes there was a man strapped into that chair and sometimes there wasn't. I walked by it once and a man was attached to it. You couldn't see what he looked like because they pulled a kind of hat down over the eyes of the ones they had sit there. The hat looked like it was a slop bucket had a brim. He didn't have any shirt on and you could see the shape of his ribs. Had the stove-in chest of a boy long been sickly, and a ugly cut hadn't healed too well straight across his stomach. They had tied a gag on his mouth. Hadn't handed him any flower to hold either.

You would have thought in that place they kept me for all those months straight through wintertime I would have done the bigger cut of my thinking about home and Bartholomew and that baby boy we had had for those cold minutes and my mother lying done with her shame in her bones beneath the ground, but the truth is I thought more about Neva Thatcher and the Colonel. That place and its ways must have stole into my head to haunt me because the two of them had come to form a kind of happy couple in my mind, Neva Thatcher with her chinaware and linden-berry mouth, the Colonel with his long whiskers and his smoke.

'Bring me Neva Thatcher,' I would tell the keeper, who would cuff me hard for it. 'Bring the Colonel,' I would yell out to the doctor when he peeped in. They did not bring Neva Thatcher to me. But one February morning with the snow falling, my Colonel came.

They took me down to a room looked like it belonged to another building altogether. It had a green and yellow rug with dogs and diamonds on it and purple wallpaper with thin red stripes. They had a table with a glass vase full of dried flowers sitting in its center and there were two soft chairs. There was a fire crackling nice on one end. A guard stood at attention but the Colonel told him it was all right and he stepped outside. There was a little window in the room and you could see the snow fall past it. While I looked at the snow, the Colonel took up the glass vase of flowers and set it on the floor.

'Gallant Ash,' the Colonel said.

'Colonel, sir,' I said back.

He suggested we move the chairs closer to the fire and sit. I was in my thin dress and expect I had let my teeth clack when I spoke to him. When we had settled he told me that his regiment had been broken to bits and scattered. Some of what was left, including him, had been redeployed.

'How is your cousin?' I said.

'Past all care,' he said.

'I am sorry.'

'I appreciate it.'

He did not look grand and gray any longer. He looked old. Like the fist of years had found out his face and struck a sure blow. There was mud upon his boots. His nose gave a trickle. His coat had a long tear down one side.

'I'm no spy,' I said.

'I understand you give out shaves to the men here,' he replied.

'Did they tell you I get to carry out the slops too?'

'They did.'

We looked a little at each other.

'I'm told I'm to be made a general,' he said.

'I gave no secrets. I did my duty.'

'Do you know what I was before this war?'

I shook my head.

'Nor do I. I cannot remember. Or if I can, it seems like a life that belongs to some other and I do not credit it. There is a wife loves me and whom I love in that life. I expect that if I am not killed, I will remember it again someday.'

'I remember my home. I remember every inch and mile. I have a husband back home waiting for me.'

'Is he? Waiting for you, I mean?'

'Why wouldn't he be?'

'I have heard it said you hail from the South. I don't believe that. Not even for one Secesh minute. Your surprise lay elsewhere. Do you remember when we spoke of surprises?'

'I am no spy. Sir, I just wanted to fight. I just wanted to go away for a while.'

'That's two different things.'

'It's one thing.'

'Explain to me how it is one.'

'I'll answer to just about any order you give me, but not that one.'

He looked at me. Long and hard.

'Because you won't or because you can't?'

'Both.'

'All right. Well, enough. Let's leave off that. Leave epistemology be. Let's return to our earlier line, which was ontological. Do you follow me?'

'No.'

'Epistemology concerns knowledge. Ontology concerns what we are.'

'Or what we aren't.'

'Not a whore, we know that, and not a spy, we know that too; that leaves only lunacy for the cause. Or at least that is what the doctor here told me. He says you suffer from that ancient malady. You have been set adrift by the moon. You gallop among the stars.'

'I don't answer to any sickness such as that.'

'I'm quoting your physician.'

'I just wanted to fight. To plant my foot and stand stalwart and never run.'

'But you did steal food and tobacco and sundry medical supplies out of the haversacks of active Federal combatants and so deprive men-at-arms, sometimes wounded men-at-arms.'

'I was a man-at-arms. Wounded for the cause.'

'You were a common thief.'

'I stole from no one.'

'It was a foul rumor, then. Nothing more. Of course it was. I know that. We have already discussed it.'

The fire gave a pop when he said this and a log shifted. The Colonel reached over, took the poker, and gave the works a push. When he leaned forward I saw he had a long scar went from his neck up the side of his face.

'You got yourself a scratch.'

'Nothing more. But I spent thirty days on furlough. Did me a world of good. My wife is the finest woman in the world. You see, I can remember her now. She appears before me. Floats there in the fireplace. You will have to meet her one of these times.'

'I would like to go home.'

'Does a body good to be home. My kinsman would have liked that. He would have liked to be shut up safe again in his rooms.'

I did not recognize the way the Colonel was looking at me. There was a difference to him, like his eyes had changed color, gone from brown to blue, or like he had lost an arm and was studying on how to take up using his left hand.

'I should have made you a sharpshooter,' he said. 'Perhaps it would have put stealing out of your mind.'

'Stealing wasn't my central transgression.'

'Then you do admit to it.'

'I would like to go home. I would go straight home if I were let to leave. I would like to write a letter to my husband. He would come and fetch me. I know they release people out of here to their families. I never stole. Or betrayed.'

The Colonel stood and put a hand on my shoulder.

'You need to wear more and better, Gallant Ash. I'll see to it that you get something else to wear. Your dress is too thin. It won't do for this cold weather. You should change clothes.'

I started to stand but he told me to sit by the fire a few more minutes.

'We must not let this war deprive us of all comforts,' he said. He bent and picked up the vase and set it back on the table. I watched his back, then turned and saw that he had left behind a letter for me.

'My Dearest Constance,' it read.

*I write you with your former name because I have grown afraid that you are no longer with us but have gone away far from this earth and its trials and its cares. It seems to me in such sad possible circumstance that I must write to you as you are and not as you seem if this letter and thought is to have any hope of reaching you. I am well, dear one, but my troubles here, previously described, continue: Now they have burned the seed shed and taken off both our mules. They want our land and continue their depredations and worsen it with talk of paving the way for the forces of the rebellion that must come. Secessionists in our midst. If I hadn't heard it from their own mouths I wouldn't have credited it. But I keep the old musket handy and walk vigilant as you would and, though they are strong, hope still to gain the upper hand. And hope too, even if I cannot prevail, to otherwise see things through. I pray that wherever you are, war or no war, this will reach you and send you, all past troubles put behind us, sailing back to me.*

I did sail home to my Bartholomew. That very night in a dream I went rushing over the treetops, along the rivers, through the chill of the mountains, spiriting north and west through snow and thunderstorm and into a white sun. I found the house burned to the ground and Bartholomew run off far away. In his place were old and evil men sharpening their plows and planning to set our good oxen to the yoke and, to the tune of 'Dixie' made it worse, gobble everything up.

It was these same men had burned our neighbor out those years before and so my mother came into the dream and stood in the center of the cinders of our house, which had been her house, and wept. The tears of my mother must have found a way out of the dream and onto my face because when I woke there they were. Hot and heavy ghosts come to haunt my face. I roared and raged then. I beat my hand and head on the door until both were bloody.

'I must go home,' I yelled. 'You must let me leave.'

It was the keeper gave me my answer. She came in hard with two buckets had ice floating on their tops. February or not, she turned them both over me. She came at me with her foot a minute later as I lay gasping and shivering, and I caught it and twisted and threw her down. The others around me laughed and cheered as I put my fists to the keeper's face. The guard came into it and I worked on him too.

'I will fight you all until you let me leave,' I said. Around me the ladies howled. One of them picked up the guard's slouch hat and did a march around the cell. When the keeper tried to get up I put my foot on her neck. It took another guard running down the hall and hitting me on the back of the head with his rifle butt to stop me.

I had many an occasion to dream about home in the long hours afterward when I woke and found they had put me in the chair. I spent two days on its rough planks with the brimmed bucket on my head, and when they untied me, I took up a candlestick and hit the doctor had finally come to visit in the face with it, so they gave me three more. A fever found me that second suite of days. To this fever I attribute the fact that although I sat in that chair the whole time, it felt to me like I was able to stand up out of myself and walk down the corridors of the madhouse and out the door and across the burning countryside. I saw soldiers at their cards or guns as I walked; I saw cannon sitting black in its iron; I saw mules and horses hadn't eaten in days hollering out in Latin for their feed. I tried one of these times to walk home but the rivers grew wide and deep and the forest grew dark and thick. I turned back to the battle then. The world was afire with it. I looked everywhere for a gun but couldn't find one. The dead spoke to me on those walks. With mouths that floated above their own bodies with the flies. They clambered up to the rafters of barns and yelled down at me from the treetops, dangled by their knees from the clouds. On one misty field an army of cats had come out to lick the corpses. The cats walked upright and carried colored banners. When I got up close to them they all turned at the same time and looked at me so I ran. Running, I found my way to a fight. The fighters had gotten their coats all mixed up and just stood in a mess trying to figure out which way they needed to turn their guns. 'Tell us a story so we'll know which way to shoot,' they said. They handed me a flower. I took it and put it between my teeth, then pointed to the steeple of a nearby church.

In between these excursions, I would come back to the chair and the bucket with its brim. There was attendants who would come along every now and again to hit the side of the bucket with a hand or poke me sharp in the ribs with a stick. They kicked me too and tightened my cords and whispered that they hoped I wouldn't wake up any longer, that they could toss me into the field nearby when I was done. They were doing that on one of my bucket walks. Carrying the blackened carcasses out to pile up in a field. I helped in the chore. Laughed until my teeth fell out. Felt the ache in me everywhere, as the job never seemed to get done. So that when after three days my keepers untied me and drenched me down with water and scrubbed me off, I hurt on every square inch of my body and did not have the strength to fight. I lay sick to dying for two weeks afterward. Puddle of arms and legs, bits of burning skin. I kept hoping I would travel out again, even if it was just to pile corpses, but it couldn't be done. It was into March before I was sitting up against the brick wall and eating the blows they fed us again.

I do not like much to think of the days that followed. When the keeper came at me I cringed and cried. When the doctor peeped in and asked me my name I told him one I had heard in a dream. I told him that I was a runaway from Chattanooga. That I had spied for the forces of the rebellion. That I had handed over secrets had led to the death of ten thousand men. The two women had once been heavy saw an advantage during these days and stole my food. The ones against the wall hollered at me and shook their chains. The women who wrung their hands looked on and shook their heads.

I cringed and groveled and scraped and moaned. The keeper smiled a gummy smile and said it was the chair had changed me. She said sometimes it took a while but that they all eventually changed. She wouldn't hold my fists and feet against me. She'd had worse. She had known a gal had thought she had invisible arms growing out of her neck had come after her with a broken bottle and cut her three times. That gal had spent one month and two days in the chair and had been cured without a trace of her previous ailment. Had never spoke of it again. All the ones chained to the wall had taken their turns in the chair and had quieted considerably after it. There was others, she said, looking around at the rest of the cohort, that could stand to try the cure.

After this speech on the virtues of the chair, she said I might get back to carrying the slop jar and giving out shaves if I continued to improve. I told her that she was right, that the chair was a wonderful thing, that I was better, that I promised to be good. I was saying this to her when I saw who the guard was standing behind her. I blinked and scrunched my eyes to see if he would go away but there still stood the Akron boy that wasn't dead.

He was on duty two weeks later when the keeper let me carry the slop jar again. She walked along with us all the way there and all the way back, though it was her custom, when this errand was made, to take her meal and sit quiet in her closet. I did not speak to the Akron boy and he did not speak to me. I had watched him and studied up on whether his months and weeks of battles had put some iron would work against my cause into him. I had watched to see if he still had a shake to his hand and a nervous-sparrow hop to his eyes. When one of the women who wrung her hands asked him if he had seen her darling boy in the fights, he did not answer but he did gulp and look away, and when, in that retreat, his eyes found mine and jumped like they had had yellow-jacket stingers shoved into their centers, I knew I could still have my hope. I carried the slops around into the alcove and the Akron boy followed me and watched me dump the slops into the trench. I took a while at emptying the jar, set it down between pours, wiped my brow. It was a horror what went slopping its way down the stream but I lingered there, made it look like I couldn't move too quick, needed minutes, not seconds, if

159

anyone was looking on to get up to a trick or two with my handsome guard.

The next week the keeper went back to her meal and her rest but the Akron boy walked behind me and I did my emptying duties exactly the same. I got some help on how it would work best to proceed the day after that when the keeper came in to see us. She was in a foul mood – tripped over my leg and gave me a rich portion of good, sharp smacks. The Akron boy was standing behind her. I did not say a word. After a time he coughed and gulped and said maybe I'd had enough. The keeper turned on him, still kicking, and asked how it was any of his affair. I was a wildcat and needed my kicks. The Akron boy said he had known me once. This set the keeper, whose mind ran with the slop trench, to chuckling and she gave me one more good kick and said she bet I was tasty. The Akron boy turned the color of the freshest autumn apple when she said this. He got so red it changed the color of the floor and the walls.

'Thank you,' I told him the next week we went out with the slops.

'You are welcome, Gallant Ash,' he said.

'You took my part and I appreciate that.'

'There was a time I wouldn't have had to. You don't seem as sturdy as you used to.'

'No,' I said. 'I expect I'm not. You look like you've found your muscles though.'

That blush came back to his face when I said this. Likely it was the size of the lie that helped turn his color. He hadn't found his muscles. He looked like he had been turned out of a prison camp last week. There wasn't any muscle on him at all.

The fourth week he was not there and I feared he had been detailed away. I was sick to retching when the fifth week came and still he had not returned. It was a big fellow gave me a jab or two with his musket who followed me down to the alcove. It was evil cold that day so I got away with only a bad minute of him standing too close and breathing on me with his foul breath.

'We'll talk on it closer next time,' he said.

On the sixth week, though, I got pushed down to the yard by the keeper to do some shaving for the first time since I'd sat in the chair and there the Akron boy was, leaning against a wall. Heaven drips down its gifts. It was five or six of them, though not the Akron boy, there for my services, in their shirtsleeves, and as I shaved the first one, the one who'd breathed hard on me the week before, he said, 'Now, don't you go and cut my throat,' and I said, 'No, sir, I won't,' and he said, 'Because I've heard you're a fierce one.' I shaved through them all, taking my time at it, looking from minute to minute at the Akron boy leaning slumped over some against the far wall.

'What about him?' I said when I had pulled my rag off the last one.

'Him?' said my bad breather. 'Shave's not what he needs.'

'Let him have a shave,' said another.

161

'He looks like he needs it,' I said.

'There's plenty he needs.'

'He's coming back, though.'

'Shave would do him good.'

'Did it do you good?'

'Plenty good.'

They went on like this awhile and then I found the Akron boy sitting in front of me. He wouldn't speak and looked ashamed. I chalked it up to the teasing.

'I haven't seen you in some while,' I said.

'He's been otherwise entertained,' said the bad breather. This made all the others laugh.

The Akron boy didn't have much beard but it was more than he had had when we had sat down together and taken our shaves in the long ago. More and plenty. I had only one brown rag to dip in and out of the big bucket of cooling water they had but I let it sit on his face a good while. When I took it off I thought I saw some smile in his eyes.

He came back to slop-jar guard duty the next day, looking even paler without his beard than he had the day before, and as we started our walk down to the alcove, I asked after his health. He told me he had been down with a wound wouldn't heal and a sick headache come along to offer the wound its company. The wound wasn't old but the sick headache he had had to confront since his earliest days. I expressed my sympathies, found a way to touch him a half a second on his hand, told him I was sorry about the teasing he had taken, asked him if he had enjoyed his shave. He did his blush again and quivered his lip and looked at my fingers and said that the following week he expected to be redeployed out to the western front; some of the ones had teased him, including the bad breather, had already left. I said that the western front sounded like it was far away.

'About as far away as it gets,' he said.

'We were about that far away in that house in the woods,' I said.

'I expect that's true.'

'You can't get any farther away from the world than the borders of the bleak beyond.'

163

It was cool even though we were getting good into spring-time, and the Akron boy had on his long coat. It dragged a little on the ground behind him and he walked with his musket held slack. I gandered back in his direction when I talked. He had a dreamy look in his eye. He was a boy should have been fishing a creek, not standing guard in a prison madhouse.

'How is that old Colonel of ours now?' I asked.

'Not a colonel anymore. He got made a general. Sits in the big camp over yonder.'

'Well, the world just turns and turns.'

'They say he talks to himself. I haven't seen it.'

'Don't we all do that?'

'I don't.'

'No, probably you don't. You look solid.'

'You think so? I been working at it. I wish you would tell them that.'

'Tell who that?'

He didn't answer me. Just looked a little more lost in his big coat.

I set the jar down, readjusted my grip, and picked it back up again. A rain was now making brown splotches on the dirt around us. There was a sleeping dog under an empty wood shelf and a pair of chickens in a twig cage by the far wall about dead and heading for someone's soup. 'That was quite a trick I played out there in the woods on those Secesh wanted to eat us for their supper, wasn't it?' I said as we rounded the corner, putting us out of sight of the building, and stepped toward the trench. There was a kind of roof over the alcove, and the rain acted like it was fixing to drum it down.

'Yes, it sure was, Gallant Ash,' he said.

'They don't call me that here,' I said.

He didn't answer, just looked at me, his head tilted a little and his mouth open like you see sometimes on the dead. I stepped out into the rain, emptied the slops like it was real work for me, then came back under the roof and turned to him.

'You want to see how I did it?' I said, lowering my voice. 'See me drop off my clothes? We got time. No one'll notice. You want to see it done?'

He was quiet and had gone all autumn-apple-colored again but there was a minute I thought I'd misjudged him. There was a minute I thought he had aged up to go with that scrub beard of his I'd shaved off and was going to work his scrawny arms and lift his gun. I thought he was going to fire it at me and that I would fall down the slop hole and get stuck or splatter off down the stream. I think it was the pleasure I should have felt at this prospect but didn't that brought me back, made me move.

I said, 'I know you didn't know all those days what it was I had hiding in my shirt. You know why I signed up? So I could get next to men, men like you.'

He coughed and gulped. He shook his head and bit at his lip. He kicked one of his boots against the other. He opened his mouth and tried to swallow. But he set his musket against the wall.

'Lean in close, now, and you can learn all the trick of it you like,' I said.

I had the wooden lid to the slop jar still in my hand. He set his tongue along his lips, leaned in close to my shoulder. I reached up with my free hand and ran a finger across his smooth cheek, then I swung up with the other and hit him hard.

'All you do for this trick,' I told him as I started unbuttoning his coat, 'is change your clothes. You take yours off and put other ones on. Let's try it now. You and me together. See how it works.'

So it was him wore the thin dress and walked in front with the empty slop jar as we went back. I had fixed his bayonet and bought his attention with a gentle slice to his side. I had told him if he so much as gave out a shiver as we went back to the cell I would put an end to his days. Like I had put an end to those outlaws we'd left in the woods.

'I never meant any harm,' he said.

'No, I expect you probably didn't,' I said.

We walked. We passed a soldier or three but they were ones I hadn't seen before and none gave us the barest look. I well knew how to walk like a man, and the Akron boy in my dress with his long golden locks made a maiden fairer than I. The keeper was on her chair in her room dozing over her coffee and porridge and did not raise her head as we passed. I put the Akron boy in the cell with the women, put a shackle on his leg, made him give me every countersign he knew, then tied a rag around his mouth. Even when he waved his arms at me and I saw again the angry wound on the top muscle of his left arm that I had already seen when I had made him undress in the yard, and that I would see in dreams to come, and can see again to this day, I did not waver. I yanked his mouth rag snug and left him there to wait. To wait to be stripped again of his guard duties, to be put back in the chair, marched out on his own bucket dreams, go back to the men's quarters they had let him emerge from a minute, and moan out his fresh tale of woe.

'You tell them over there that Gallant Ash sends his regards,' I whispered at him.

*Don't leave me here like this,* his eyes spoke back.

One of the heavy gals wasn't heavy anymore came over at me when I was standing up from tying his rag, and I took a minute to pay her and her friend back for having stolen my food. The keeper, for her part of it, got the musket butt to the side of her head. I had not eaten in two days so I gobbled down what she hadn't eaten of her porridge and drank her coffee and, before I left, sat a minute on her chair.

I expect anyone just come out of that place would have run about as fast as he could for the hills but run is not what I did. Instead, I walked out slowly through the front door, past the sleepy guards posted there, gave them each a good grin, got back a brace of grins in return, shouldered my new Springfield, and set off down the road and out of the town where the sick house was and back to the one where Neva Thatcher had her quiet little home. I passed many a footsore soldier along the way. They just nodded at me or asked for news, but I shook my head and said I had none to give. One fellow louder than the others called out about the Wilderness fight and how so many wounded boys had died of fire and not their wounds. There was a picket detail on the bridge led into Neva Thatcher's town who liked the countersign I gave them and let me through. They had a battle going somewhere nearby and I went through town with an ammunition convoy dragged by tired, hoof-cracked mules.

The battle going on must have been somewhere picturesque without any burning boys to it because there was a party of handsome-dressed fancy people carrying field glasses fixing to ride out to inspect it. The oldest man of the group gave me a right smart nod when I went by, like he was looking forward to seeing me fight a little later in the day. I nodded back, then crossed through the mule train to the other side of the street. A little later I crossed back over and walked up the path and around the back and into Neva Thatcher's house.

You could hear the battle about as well inside as you could outside but inside it was warm and neat. The old kind of quiet made of mists and dust-gloom reigned there. Neva Thatcher had her breakfast cup drying on the sideboard, and a pile of apples waiting to help get her through the week. She had salt pork and hardtack sitting next to a lump of lard in the cupboard. A stone jug of cool water from her well. In the side room I found her underthings and dresses folded neat. I chose a green-colored gown and a pair of sturdy shoes couldn't have fit me much better and made a bundle of them with the food I had recruited from the kitchen. Then I went to the dining room.

The chinaware was dusted fresh, its flowers and animals sleeping quiet. Some of the afternoon sun was thieving in through the blinds and nibbling at it. There were motes adrift in the light. I lifted up a hand through some of it and made them swirl. I took up Neva's grandaunt's teapot by its handle, carried it to the dining table, lifted it, and started to bring it down. I had had it in my mind the whole walk there to break her chinaware and lay the broken pieces across her floor but holding the pretty thing in my hand, I found I could not do it and instead simply carried the teapot to her room and set it

169

on her pillow. There where she laid her linden-berry head and dreamed her linden-berry dreams. She helped the wounded, shepherded the sick. She had helped me. Then she hadn't. There it was. I could feel it. I had it again. I knew where she kept a mallet and I fetched it out and went back to her room and I pounded the china-pot heirloom on her bed pillow until its powders were floating up into the air. After I had finished, I stood awhile in front of the rest. Picked up one of the monkey plates. Thought some more. But in the end I put down the plate, dropped the mallet, and left Neva Thatcher's house.

I went next to the camp outside of town. The pickets were down and I walked right through the camp and a few hundred yards more along a corduroy road to the rear line. Some of the mules I had walked with earlier were just shambling up. I passed a group of cooks playing poker with a second lieutenant in the shade of an apple tree. Men in reserve waiting to see if they would have a turn on the front line that day were dozing in the sun. I still had my coat on, and one or two eyed me a little closer than I liked so I took it off. There was a tall major wearing a stovepipe hat looked a minute like Abraham Lincoln who was swearing at his mount. The wounded were already coming through the trees. I saw one boy crawling with a slick of blood emerging from the corner of his mouth. Every couple of feet he would cough and the slick would spread. There were tears on his dusty cheeks. He kept looking around him and calling out for water. He was crawling to a grave would open up any minute and it made me tired to look at him so I went up to the rise where I had seen the commander's flag.

My Colonel now a General had his desk set up in front of a day tent. He had left off the start of a letter addressed to Yellow Springs, Ohio, to go to his duty. I picked up this start to a letter and put it down. All he had had time to write on it was the words *My Dear*. There wasn't anywhere a soul not seeing to some business, and not one of those souls spoke to me. Down the hill there was a rebel charge. We had guns set on the high ground and blew it, by the sound of screaming afterward, to rough bits. I set the overcoat on the General's chair and tore off the bottom half of his piece of paper. I took up his pen and wrote *Found myself something warmer to wear* on one line, and on the next, *just like you told me I should,* and I set the paper on top of the overcoat. Then I laid down my borrowed musket, walked away from that battle and that camp, found some bushes, and changed my clothes.

# THREE

That afternoon I slept my way until dusk time in a cave in a hickory tree had been hollowed out to smoke meat. There were some meat shreds caught in the wrinkles and crevices of the wood, and my fingers found them and felt of them and brought them to my mouth. I woke at moonrise with my teeth chattering hard enough to crack hickory nuts and set off at a trot up the road to try and get warm. I wasn't any ways at all up the road when I come up on another traveler, a colored gal I knew straight off I had seen before, though it took me a minute to know where. She was taller than me and broader at the shoulder. She walked like she wasn't back in a dress. Maybe she had always walked that way. Down in a field. Hundred-pound basket on her back. It came to me. The last time I had seen her she had been marching out of our camp wearing contraband pantaloons.

'You can come on out of the shrubbery,' I said, for she had vanished as quick as spit as soon as I came up on her. I called this out more than once. I called it out and told her I wasn't going to alert the guard or the dogs or anything. I said I knew she was hiding in the bushes not even an apple throw away and that she ought to quit being scared and come out. Or if

175

she couldn't quit being scared she ought to come out anyway. I was heading north, I said, and if she liked, we could be two travelers together on the road instead of two travelers apart. I said all of this and felt like I was making quite a fair speech out there in the dark night but it wasn't until I told her I knew she had been a man and that I had been one too that she came up out of the bushes. She was even bigger standing next to me than she had looked hurrying along the chalky road. We hung there some time not saying any word then settled kind of gradual into walking. She was dressed in heavy skirts and a shawl. She had a rag bundle in one hand and a heavy stick in the other.

'Have you had anything to eat?' I said.

She shook her head so I fetched her up a cracker. It took some time of me holding it out and us walking along for her to take it. It took even more of us walking down the road and past a frozen pond and through a grove of burned trees holding up their empty devil hands at the dark for her to lift it up to her mouth and crunch.

'What regiment?' she said.

I told her and when she said she'd shouldered her rifle awhile for the Fifth U.S. Colored I asked her why she had stopped.

'Why did you stop?' she said.

I gave out a cough started out as a laugh at how long it would take me to answer and we left it there at that.

After a minute and another bite of wilty cracker she said,

'After Antietam, that's where I saw you,' and I said that was right and something a little like a smile come up in her eyes but it didn't stay there long.

'I thought you were a ghost coming along that road back there,' she said.

'I'm not a ghost,' I said. 'I don't think I'm a ghost.'

'Ghost of my old mistress come along the road to catch me. Left her dead of a finger went sour back in South Carolina. She came to me all through the fighting, pointing at me with that finger.'

I showed her my fingers. She nodded. She also shivered a little and you could see plain it wasn't a shiver come from the cold.

'I've seen a ghost,' I said. 'I think I did.'

She nodded. Kind of sucked up her lips.

'My ghost had a knife.'

'Ghosts don't need knives.'

'Mine did.'

She looked away to the side, shook her head.

'You got to get north and out of this country,' I said. 'We could help each other, share the road.'

'Share the road,' she said. If she had been a well you could have dropped a stone down her throat and not heard any echo.

We kept walking, with her some way in front or some way behind, and after some good yards of this I started to talk. I had it in my mind, I suppose, to cheer us a little along the way after our talk about ghosts, maybe pull a story or two out of her, hear something about her own fighting days, march along together like two soldier men, even if we were wearing dresses, but the stories I told were about as twisted up as wet turkey feathers and she just kept breathing in and breathing out and looking back and forth across the road. I told one about Antietam, because we had both of us been in those parts, deep in those ugly times, about an unscratched lieutenant had done well for his men in the fight and when it was over leaned his head against a hot cannon barrel and burned off his ear. That story had seemed funny to me at one time but it didn't any longer out there on the road in the moonlight, so I told another meant to be rosier about a Confederate boy so hungry he tried to play bear and got himself stung to death scooping up fresh honey. When we come up on him, I told it, he had gotten so swollen you could have rolled him down a hill like a ball. There was an old lady had a corncob pipe stuffed in her mouth sitting there next to him said she had some claim on this bee-stung boy, though what claim that could have been I do not know because we didn't ask. We left her sitting there with her legs splayed out, waiting for him to swell back down. He had something of hers in his pockets, she told us as we walked away, and the swelling had stretched them too tight and she couldn't fetch her hand in. I gave a chuckle when I told this story but my fellow wanderer didn't think as much of it as I did.

'The hell kind of story is that to tell?' she said.

'You ever pretend like you needed a shave?' I asked.

'A shave?'

Thinking about shaves set me to thinking about Bartholomew and I told my companion about the beard that wouldn't ever grow very well on his face, though maybe, I said, during the many months that had galloped past, he had learned the beard-growing trick. I told her about Bartholomew's small hands and how he was a better operator in the kitchen with his small hands than I was with mine. I told her that he had a bottle of French cologne water that he liked to sprinkle on a handkerchief before he went out of a morning to do his work. I had missed him terribly, I told her, and more all the time. I was going home to him now, to reacquaint myself with him after the hard separation and set things straight on our farm and settle scores.

'What kind of scores?' she said.

She said this and it seemed to me that a new note of interest had crept into her voice and I would otherwise have leaped in to tell her what I meant but we both heard that very minute horse hooves on the trail behind us and so we stepped quick and quiet off the road.

'They had me locked up,' I whispered as we crouched in the frosty bushes. 'There was a chair they put me in. A bucket they put over my head. This dress I got on is borrowed. Ain't impossible that I'm being chased. You got anyone in particular after you?' She didn't answer, just looked long at me and then long at the road and the horses filled it up, then left it

179

empty again. I don't know why it is I got that image of a road empty of us and of anything else but the moon making a white ribbon of it stuck in my head.

'You want to hear about those scores now? I got all kinds of them,' I said after a time.

'We used to kill dogs,' she said.

'Kill dogs?' I said.

'Every one of them we could in those last days. I beat one of those bloodhounds to death with a butter churn.'

I thought about it a minute. It came to me then that I'd heard stories about dogs had had their throats slit on the big spreads, dogs dead the way she'd said and wouldn't go hunting runaways anymore.

'We ought to go on now, the road is clear,' I said.

She again didn't answer but there had been a shift in her shoulders and suddenly I didn't like the look of the size of her as we crouched there in the dark. I tried to stand but the next second I found myself with her knee on my chest and her stick across my throat.

'Tell you what,' she said.

I fought halfway up and she wrestled me back down and got her knee and stick pressed down harder. There's times part of me likes to think if I hadn't been fresh out of the slops and ice baths I could have fought her but there's the other part of me thinks there just wasn't any way I ever could have.

'You want to share the road, head up north together, we both wore the blue, fought the grays, well, tell you what,' she said.

'Tell you what. It's a winter's day. January day. You feel the cold of the ground here, that's just the swaddling to the cold of the day I'm conjuring. There's rain coming down, rain like the ropes of the draper man. Ruts and puddles in the barn-yard. The one rooster whose neck you haven't wrung hasn't crowed day yet. So it's darker than this dark we got here. It's black-cold and wet and you got little ones on their pallets and your old mother still dreaming in her chair. Your old mother who never did anything but work and get whipped every day you've been alive. Dreaming her dreams. You tell me where she was. Where those dreams had made her go. It's cold like that and it's dark like the devil's teeth and you are awake because you just heard the warning bell. Death is coming down the road to knock on your door and you don't know what to do. Master's back after barely a month from the war and Mistress is dead of her bad finger and lies in the dirt next to her dead sons and now he's coming to bury you. Bury you and your babies and your old mother before he'll let you go to live with Uncle Lincoln up north. Live in his white house and pluck fruit from his trees. Master and his hired boys are coming. I got two arms and one back. I got three babies and one old mother can't walk. "Run now" is what my old mother said. She got up long enough to get one of my babies on my back and snug the other two into my arms. "Run now," she said. My old mother. There was a rise across the yard with bushes like these ones and I went there and I watched them come and pull my old mother out by her hair into the yard. Make her lie down in one of the puddles. Hold her down there in the wet. Hold her down there until she didn't move. Me carrying three babies. Sitting there watching them drown my mother. Like a rat to spit on. And any minute any one of my babies might cry. And you want to share my road? Hand me a cracker and help me on my way? Tell me stories about some fool captain and some other fool got his pockets swollen shut? Shaves and French perfume?'

'I fought them,' I said, even though that stick at my neck hadn't budged, even though I couldn't breathe, even though I thought I was looking up into the eyes of my end.

'Not them, you didn't,' she said. 'You didn't fight any of that,' she said. 'You did not,' she said, putting her face down almost nose to nose with mine, her mouth almost onto mine, her shoulders almost onto my own, 'fight any inch of that.'

'Where are your babies?' I said.

'My what?'

'I had a baby once.' I don't know why I said that to her.

She didn't answer, just took the knee off my chest and the stick off my neck and set off into the dark woods behind us. Away from the moon-white ribbon of the empty road. Last thing I heard her say as she vanished and I lay there choking up the air could now come back at last into my throat was 'Tell you what.'

When I was young, my mother liked to start one story and finish it off with another. Hansel and Gretel would end with Rumpelstiltskin, and the Snow Queen with Mother Hen. I don't know if she did this to investigate my state of interest or awakeness or because she thought the old tales had gotten played out and she wanted to freshen them up. Sometimes she would put three or four together. Tie them into a bundle and let loose the whole shooting match. Bartholomew claimed to me once he had heard her at this game but I don't know how he could have since she was dead of her own hand no time at all after he gave me that dark red zinnia I took in the house and pressed and have lying here in its hints of old-time crimson even now. Maybe he dreamed it. Maybe my mother visited him in his sleep. Maybe she talked to him too. Told him about the gingerbread boy ran out of the house and bit an apple and the little man spun gold so the whole kingdom fell asleep, the end.

Whether Bartholomew had dream visitors or sat one night outside our window and heard my mother stitching stories together or he didn't, I had moments after I left the rebellious states and as I walked and rode my slow way back to our

Indiana farm that I thought I had stepped out of one story and into some other. In that other I was now in, the angel of death had not unfurled its wings and blacked out the stars and sent metal and men to shriek together in its awful night wouldn't ever end. Here where I now walked there were no fields of fresh dead to sink in up to your knees, no bee-stung boys in gray or blue or any of the other colors you could find on the field, no towns entire gone mad, no hot cannon, no dogs beat to death with butter churns. Instead there was a season full of flowers, fields that felt the plow and fat young cows at their grass. Birds swooped the trees and sang the branches. Lee's try on Pennsylvania was long since just bones for the ages in the fields. Laundry hung sweet on the line. Clocks ticked loud on mantels and told something like the right time.

My hair had grown and I had on Neva Thatcher's good dress and good shoes and more than one family took me in for a meal. It was times strange enough and they did not ask me why I was abroad. A pair of sisters I dinnered with said they had given soup to a trio of one-armed jugglers not the week before. An old man and woman in a house at the bottom of an apple orchard outside Waynesburg had woken up one morning to find a stove-in mortar abandoned in their barn. Negroes done forever with the South and its yokes were everywhere with their bundles and mules. I thought I recognized my friend from the road one time. But it was some other woman dressed in rag skirts with a calico swaddle in each of her strong arms. Here and there you would cross a

185

discharged veteran still had bombs and bullets flying in his eyes but there was good swaths of the country been emptied out of its men. Didn't stop the ones who were still there or already back from trying out their tricks and evils, though. It was them more than once let me know my story hadn't yet slipped its hinges entirely into some other one.

The first time I was just over into eastern Ohio and had been marching a stretch in the rain. Yonder I saw light in a house and I went up and knocked on its door. There was a big fellow with a scar on his forehead come to answer. He told me to step in, step in, said I looked hungry and his wife would get me my supper. The wife looked to be about seventy-five pounds of beat-up bone. She had a bright blue bruise on her cheek and didn't say a word, only gave out a cringe when the husband pointed a finger at her. When the husband stepped past – to get some cider, he told me, from the shed – she gave me up a hand gesture you didn't have to work too hard to understand meant *run*. I stayed long enough to look out the window and see it wasn't cider he was bringing back from the shed but a standard U.S. military–issue horse pistol and a length of rope. I told the woman she ought to come with me but she just smiled at this, handed me a biscuit, and said she wasn't worried for herself. I stepped out the kitchen door and trotted off with my biscuit into the dark and rain. I gnawed that biscuit under a lilac bush. The woman had dipped it into some lard and it made a fair meal. As I chewed I thought about her bruise. The rain came down hard through the lilac.

I don't know why I was sitting under it. There is shelter and then there is the idea of shelter. Shore up under the second all you want. You still get wet.

*I need to run on out of here and keep getting home,* I thought. I thought this once and then I thought it again. I tried saying it out loud to my mother but didn't get any answer. Tried to think of when I had last talked to her. Started to make my plan about leaving this place and marching off through the rain, marching all night. Still, when I had finished the biscuit I groped myself up a good stick and circled back as wet as a drowned piglet to the lit house. When I got there, ready to take my chances against the horse pistol, I lifted my eyes up to the window and saw the two of them sitting next to the fire. The rope lay coiled on the mantelpiece and the pistol wasn't anywhere in sight. Go on and figure. World has many ways. The man was weeping with his head in his hands, and the woman had a smile on her face and was slurping at a cup of tea.

Another less interesting time it was an old grandpa thought he needed to snatch a kiss from me. He had offered me a ride on his manure wagon and when I sat down next to him he hit me straight off in the face with the pommel of his switch. Then he tried to slobber over on top of me. I got the idea that he broke something when he hit the ground next to his mule. I drove on another few miles then left the wagon by the side of the road. The mule tried to follow me a few steps but gave up pretty quick. I had a notion lasted five minutes that I would unhitch it and ride it off for home. The thought came to me, though, about a boy out of Martins Ferry in my company had tried that once with a sutler's mule and got hung up by his thumbs for three hours then drummed out of camp at my own Colonel's now a General's order when they caught him. Still, I did unhitch the mule and give it a good swat to get it going out over the fields and away from that old man, though. There was more than just the sting of the old man's crop over my eyebrow to motivate me. More than just the man those days before with his rope and horse pistol. More than the memory of all the men I'd lived my life with in the Union army. Men who would piss on a dying cat. Laugh at a little boy lost. Violate a woman in her autumn years. Burn a house belonged to church ladies. Lock you up in the mad chamber and leave you there to rot.

No, I unhitched that mule and sent it flying because I'd had a picture come to me of my mother. My mother tall and strong. My mother who could captain a heavy scythe all day then go out into the moonlight and plow. My mother, all of that, sitting on the front step with her head in her big hands, her shoulders a-heave, her eyes when I could look at them gone far away from me like beads of black glass. I had been out at some chore and had seen a man come up to the house. I had seen him stand talking to my mother and had seen him shaking his head and pointing his finger at her and at me even where I was way off in the distance and then walking away and climbing up onto his wagon. There had been men aplenty come up to our house for one reason or another but there hadn't been any before had left my mother sitting like that in her own puddle of tears.

I was five years old when that man came and left and didn't come back to our property for many a year. Didn't keep me from getting the fancy that I should have unhitched his animal while he was talking and pointing and turning my mother's eyes into black beads. Many was the time in the days to come, even though my mother went straight back even that afternoon to being her invincible self, that I saw it in my head how I would unhitch that man's animal and poke it with a stick. Watch it run off. Set the man maybe to chasing me. It takes work to unhitch an animal. I never could have done it. But that was the fancy that took me. And that was what I thought of there on that day as I unhitched the old man's mule. Of my mother crying. Of my fancy. Of the man I'd hear it later said was my father hollering and chasing after me.

It wasn't just time- and war-ruined men had tricks to try. Two days after I left that mule to run free I found myself at table with three young girls. I had crossed them sitting together at the end of the lane that led down to their farm. Sitting shoulder to shoulder and twisting daisy chains. Littlest one had a daisy crown in her hair, daisy bracelets around her wrists. They said hello and I said hello back.

'You hungry?' they asked me.

There wasn't any doubt by then that I was.

'Where's your folks?' I said. The biggest one winked up at the sky. The middle one smiled out over the fields.

Their father was dead at Shiloh and their mother had vanished away long ago, and now it was just the three of them. The youngest couldn't much more than talk, and the two older ones weren't any riper down the road than eight or ten. This didn't stop them from welcoming me in once we had got down their lane and serving me up a fair soup of pork and beans, nor from handing me a hunk of soft bread, a chew of butter, and a cup of good cream milk. They had a square locket had pictures of both their parents and took turnabout wearing it around their necks. It looked to be about every hour that one would take it off and pass it to the next, who would put it on, open it, give a nod, and get back to her business, whether that was handling a broom or playing with a corncob doll. The floors were swept, the windows washed, daisy chains were everywhere, and they let me lie down for the night in their parents' soft bed. When I woke the next morning all was as cheerful as the day before except that my dress and shoes were gone.

'Now you can't leave,' the oldest of them said.

'Not ever,' said the middle girl.

They had spread the table with food. There was good coffee had but just a minute before boiled. I sat down barefoot in my underthings and ate. I went barefoot in my underthings with them on their chores and took my midday dinner the same way. More than once as we walked the yard the three of them looked over at the well. I let the little one climb up into my lap as we rested a minute at midday. I gave her a tickle and told the older girls they were doing handsome by her, that if they kept on that way they would see her raised up nice. This pleased them so much they let me take a turn wearing their locket and offered me up a show after the meal. Both of them could dance and sing. The older of the two brought down a banjo had belonged to their uncle. She played it so well it made me uncomfortable to watch.

'Don't you have any family you can go to?' I asked when the show was over.

'Such as they are, they are up in Cleveland,' said the oldest.

'That's quite a way you have of talking,' I said to her.

'But we like it here,' said the middle one. 'We want to stay here forever.'

'Forever and ever,' said the youngest.

'That's a long time,' I said.

'Don't you like it here?' said the oldest.

'I do,' I said and gave the youngest another tickle. Then I walked outside, pulled the bucket up out of the well shaft, and retrieved my dress and shoes. When I had put them on I found I had the barrel of a pin-fire pistol trained on me. It was in the hands of the oldest girl. I walked over to her and placed my hands on top of hers and held them there a minute, then let them go.

'You have to fire that thing to make it work on a person,' I said.

'I know how to fire it,' she said.

I nodded and thanked the girls for their hospitality, accepted the bundle of food they had packed for me, told them I wouldn't stand for any crying or carrying on, and left off down the road.

An hour later I crashed through a small wood had set a squadron of deerflies after me and came across a place where the earth swelled up like a giant's dinner bell. There was a tree or two on the flanks of this swollen place but the ground underfoot was spongy and mostly it was just high grass and scrub. I walked up this swelling and paused on its top. I had heard about mounds like these, heard there were whole dead cities buried in each one of them, that no one now alive could say for sure how they had come to be.

I crouched a minute and scraped at the soft surface. I lay on my side with my ear to it. Sun for a blanket. Tune one of the girls had sung on my lips. The dirt below me felt heavy. Like it might whisper. Whisper some secret. I fell asleep and dreamed the world had run to its end.

I don't think I would have done anything much more than imagine a visit to Yellow Springs, Ohio, if a tinker selling bedsheets and colored socks hadn't asked me was I bound there. I hadn't been, hadn't even had any idea I was near it, but after he had taken out a sample of his wares, and I had told him I did not at that present time need anything he had to offer, even if the red of his socks was, as he had said, very fine, I followed his direction over a hill and down a good road and took myself into town.

It was a handsome place. Good, quiet streets and neat houses had squared about each one of them its own pretty yard. There was a well-made church and churchyard with more than a few fresh graves. I found the General's cousin, buried beneath pink granite and a young almond tree fluttering its first raggedy blossoms in the breeze. The stone had careful carving you couldn't see from afar. There were stars and birds. There was a bright harvest moon. If you looked close you could see a river curling off toward heaven. Under the cousin's name were his dates. Under his dates was the word *Unafraid*.

It didn't take much asking to find what had been the

cousin's house. I meant just to have my look from afar but there was the woman of the house chopping hard at some rosebushes spoke to me and told me I had to come in. I said I had been scrabbling with outlaws and orphans in the countryside and wasn't fit for stepping in a fine house, but I had known her husband and, if she liked, would sit with her a minute on her porch. She took off her garden hat, wiped a hand through her hair, sat me down, and bade me wait, then five minutes later brought out cool tea and sandwiches on soft bread. She brought a whole stack of those sandwiches, which had ham and sweet pickles swimming in fresh butter, and I worked hard at not eating them too fast. Once or twice as I ate I started to speak but she held up a hand. She was as fine to look at as her town. Into her middle years but elegant along with it, maybe more so for her age, soft and flinty both, gentle at the same time as hard. She sipped quietly at her tea and looked out over her garden. She had pink and purple hydrangeas blooming, white lilacs, a pale-trunked line of peach and apple and sour cherry trees. There were maples everywhere well into leaf and you could see the church steeple shining white beyond.

'Where did you know my husband?' she said when I had eaten the last sandwich and wiped my hands on my napkin. I didn't like for her to look at my fingers for they were nothing but dirt and chewed-down nails. Even if I had tried to scrub at them some at a well on the way over to her house.

'I knew him to look at in Maryland and Virginia and some

earlier in Kentucky too. He was about as brave as they make them. He would just stand straight up through a battle, calm and quiet. Like it was Sunday afternoon and we'd all gone home from church to eat these sandwiches of yours.'

She smiled and she shivered. You could barely tell which was which.

'He did his duty, no doubting that. There wasn't a man in his company would claim the contrary,' I said.

'Were you attached to his regiment?'

'I did laundry and sundry jobs. Drove a wagon now and again. I can cook a little if I have to. Helped the sutlers spread their wares.'

She had a sharp eye and she looked a good while at me. If I had had on my uniform, she would have seen straight past it like it wasn't there.

'And now you have left that service and walked all the way up here from Virginia?'

'I'm heading back to my husband, who stayed home for the war.'

'Ah,' she said. 'A young married woman, far from her home, traveling with an army at a time of war. That's an extraordinary image.'

'Yes, ma'am,' I said.

'Penelope gone to the war and Odysseus staying home.'

'Ma'am?'

She was quiet awhile and sipped her tea. I did the same. It was good tea. Plenty of sugar and more of mint. There was birdsong in the air. Robin. Cardinal. Wren. One or two I didn't know. Some yelling to add to it from a jay. It was a big brick house and just the porch would have done for fifty. We didn't have a porch at home, though we had often set our chins toward the subject and talked about building one.

'Please excuse me a moment,' she said.

She stood and went into the house and came back out with a green velvet sleeve. Out of this sleeve she took a gilt frame. She held it close to her. The gilt had been well wrought and looked pretty against her dark blue dress, like a window onto the other world.

'We had this likeness made before he left on his orders. He was still a professor then, finishing up his spring term.'

'A professor,' I said.

'Here at Antioch, of course. The college is shut down now. We expect it will reopen after the war. It stands just over there.' She waved toward some poplars. There was a hint of stone through the trees, a pair of peeping towers, the corner of a wall, the mossy curve of a well. She handed me the frame and asked me if her husband had still resembled his likeness. If the war hadn't ravaged his fine looks away entirely. She had seen him after he was wounded, she said, and had not liked what she saw and had begged him to stay at home with her after his recovery.

'This is your...?' I said.

'My husband,' she said.

I had in my hands a picture of the Colonel, my Colonel who had become a General.

197

'Then you are not the wife of the man lies yonder under the pink stone who was the General's cousin.'

'The General's younger brother.'

'His brother.'

'My husband called him his cousin so that the connection would not be too clear. Neither too clear nor too close.'

I sat silent. My brain making its rearrangements.

'He was not well, of course, and he would not be parted from the General. The General was good to him. Very good.'

'Very good,' I said, my brain still trying to make the new shape.

'Yes,' she said.

'Yes,' I said back.

Then I had it all. Nothing was any different.

'I never spoke to him but once; still, I saw him many a time. Like I said it a minute ago, he did his duty.'

'Just as you did yours.'

I looked at her. She had her eye on me again and was smiling. It was a kind smile. There wasn't any shivering.

'Has the General changed, in your reckoning of it?'

'Yes.'

'Yes,' she said. She crossed her feet in front of her and sipped her tea. She looked hard at me again.

'I know you did not do any laundry and wagon-driving down in Maryland and Virginia, unless it was your own laundry and the wagon-driving was in your official orders.'

I did not answer her, just sat holding the likeness of the

General carefully in one hand and my glass carefully in the other. She took a letter out of a clever pocket sewn with crimson ribbon onto the front of her dress. She unfolded it and read.

*My Dear,*
*There is a young woman who disguised herself and fought bravely and indeed with considerable distinction for a time in my regiment. She was badly treated upon her discovery. By myself not least of all. After paying me a visit earlier this afternoon to leave me a warm coat she no longer required, she is gone away from us now and I hope has left war behind forever. I do not know why I think this, and so hesitate, my dear, to write it, but I somehow expect she will be coming to you. Look for her along the road. Treat her well if she arrives. Give her your welcome. Let her know she has mine too.*

She showed me the letter and I looked a little at it. There was a brown thumbprint on the left side of the page where someone with dirty fingers had held it. The bottom half of the page had been torn off. The General had a long, tall hand looked something like he did. He had written in a kind of purple ink that bled here and there around the letters, making some of the curlicues look like chrysanthemums.

'He knew it about me long before anyone else,' I said.

'I can well imagine that he did,' she said.

'But he said nothing.'

'No, he wouldn't have.'

'Why wouldn't he have?'

'I don't know.'

'What was he a professor of?'

'Greek and Latin.'

'I am very tired.'

'Then you must come in the house, Private Thompson, and lie down.'

I stayed at the house of the General still away at war and of his wife, who was good to me, for longer than I would have thought, for the crops were up and it was deep on into summer when I started to think about setting back out on my road. I had stayed all that time in the big room that had been the General's brother's and as I began at least in my mind to step away from the house and make north and west for home, I thought considerably about his soft eiderdown and good feather bed. It had been the kind of bed you could bury yourself down into and let the warmth and softness smother your dreams. There was something about that bed had to do in my mind with the Indian mound and the chair in the madhouse and the General's brother's grave and my mother's grave and the one I had waiting for me soon or late whether I did or I didn't keep on. It was that trick of did or didn't got me slowed and looking slow one way and then the other and then no way at all. In the middle of that no way I found a bucket. Filled up with tears. The bucket was leaking. I wiped my cheeks with the pillowcase. There was some more leak came out. I had never cried beyond getting my eyes damp before. Or any good crying I had done was past my remembering of it: scrawny child in her mother's arms. I did not like that I was doing it now but couldn't see any way to stop it. My bucket was still leaking when the General's wife knocked on my door one warm late morning and told me to come down, someone needed my help.

'I fear I am indisposed, ma'am,' I told her.

'Well, dispose of your upset and come on down,' she said back.

It was a wagon with an old man looked an awful lot at first glance like my beau from the road. This man didn't have any chaw dribble in his beard, though, and when I walked up with the General's wife, he took off his hat and gave a nice nod. He was soft and green of eye to the point that they watered what looked like tiny green leaves and after I had made my own head nod back at him I could see he was missing an arm.

'I can do it all but I can't shift boxes,' he said.

'Glad to help you,' I said.

The General's wife gave us each a good smile and we left, or that's how it seemed as I thought about it later as the old man's mare went trotting along. There had been the General's wife's smile and then there was us, me and the old man, his watery eyes and my leaky bucket, and the open road leading us out of town.

'You take snuff?' the old man said, reaching into his waist pocket, pulling out a turquoise bag, and fetching out a pinch.

'No,' I said, then I said, 'Yes,' thinking it might help wake me up away from my reveries.

'Those are strong-looking hands you're wearing there,' the old man said after I had stopped my sneezing.

'My name is Constance,' I said.

'I know it,' he said. 'We got introduced back there in town.'

I didn't say anything to this and we rolled on a ways in silence, up a flower-topped hill and down its other side. The old man had been casting me quick glances with those watery green eyes and after another minute of rolling he said, 'Weatherby. Weatherby is my name.'

'Nice to meet you,' I said.

'Meet you again, is what you mean.'

We rolled some more and hit a patch of crows working a deer carcass, and Weatherby said it looked like they were having a grand time. That there was few things happier than an animal had found its midday meal. He said the General's wife had packed us sandwiches and after we had picked up our load we could have a picnic under a shade tree. There was nothing, he said, like a picnic under a shade tree, a picnic under a shade tree in the summertime couldn't be beat if you worked at it a year. Then he said if he had a handkerchief he would offer it to me. I hadn't realized it but my bucket was back at it, leaking tears out of my eyes, brown ones. Dead leaves. Creek mud. Falling down my face and off my jaw.

'I understand you've had some scare out along the road and seen some things of the war,' Weatherby said.

'I am sorry,' I said. 'I do not know myself, I do not know myself at all.'

'I lost this arm in a fight fifty years ago,' he said. 'My son is gone and my grandson is still down there in the Shenandoah.'

'Then I pity you,' I said.

'Pity the whole wide world while you're at it,' he said. 'But what I meant by that remark was that I've done my share of letting it leak out too.'

I wiped my face on my shirtsleeve. It did not strike me until later that he had used the word *leak* in referring to his tears. I did not cry ever again after those days of care and comfort in Ohio, but forever after when I saw someone at it, large or small, I thought of buckets dripping their contents.

'I thought I was turning into a crybaby,' I said when we had got a little farther and I realized my face had stayed dry.

'You don't look like any crybaby to me,' he said.

He had let the mare slow to a dull step but now he flicked the reins and we jollied on.

There were fifteen crates to be carried and we found them stacked neat in the front of a shop had been owned by a man had earned some of his living making likenesses up into the war. The machine stood with its black shawl in the center of the shop opposite a red velvet curtain hung over a vanity screen. The likeness-maker's sister, who was overseeing the

204

affair, said we could take the machine in the bargain if we wanted it but I didn't say a word and Weatherby shook his head. There was a coal-black chicken in the shop with us while we worked. It was pecking at the cork on a jug under one of the benches and didn't let anything disturb it. It wasn't any work at all to shift the crates to the wagon but Weatherby fretted some over how I stacked them in.

There were shade trees aplenty on the dead likeness-maker's property but Weatherby said that if I could wait, there was a spot he liked back down the road. We pulled up some water was warmer than it ought to have been from a well with a mossy rope and slaked off our thirst. As I held the wet well bucket in my hands, I waited a minute to see if I would start back at it but I didn't. When we were set to go, the sister came out, took Weatherby's money without a word or sign, then disappeared into the dead likeness-maker's house again.

We had our picnic under a giant crab apple had once, said Weatherby, stood beside a house that had vanished along with all of its traces from the earth. He knew of this house because he had once worked its fields, or something to that effect. Some in the neighborhood believed a tornado had picked the house up and flung it, along with a family full of children, down into Kentucky or up over the Great Lakes.

'You ever see a tornado, Constance?' he asked me.

'I saw the war is all.'

This kept him quiet a time although I hadn't meant it to

205

when I had said it. In the middle of his quiet he swallowed down a pickled carrot and walked off into the bushes. I expected he was seeing to his business and shut my eyes but when he came back some good while later he was dripping and said he had been into a pond for a swim. We had to start heading back but there was time, if I wanted, for me to take a dip. He would sit under the crab apple and crunch on carrots and make sure no one – even though he was willing to bet one of his boxes that the road would remain empty – disturbed me.

'What's in those boxes, anyway?' I said.

'Glass. For a greenhouse,' he said.

I walked through the bushes and down a twisting path that went right through the marshy middle of a stand of cattails to the edge of the water. The surface of the water was smooth except for the skaters on it. I took off my shoes and socks and hitched up my dress and stepped in, sent the skaters skittering off into the weeds. The cool from my feet and ankles rose straight up to my neck and I stepped out and wrestled off my clothes. It was when I was back in it up to my thighs, holding still and hoping the handsome skaters would return, that my mind turned a crank and I remembered my adventure in the creek. I remembered killing that rebel boy in the water after I had danced with him. Whether I had or I hadn't. Danced or killed. Fiddle music bedeviled my ears. I shuddered so hard I fell over sideways. There were fish or snakes in the wet dark and one of them brushed by my shoulder. Sleep was all I wanted. Get back to that bed at the General's house or drown. But I stayed in the water awhile longer and didn't drown. Lay there adrift on my back letting some little fish nibble at my toes.

All the ride over to Weatherby's and all the unloading and careful stacking and all the ride back to the General's house, the talk was about the war. Once Weatherby got started you couldn't get him stopped, didn't matter how long you didn't say anything, how long you swatted sweat bees away from your eyelashes or looked off into the yonder clouds.

'You were down there close up to some of those battles, if I understand it correctly,' Weatherby said. 'Don't you have an opinion?'

'I have an opinion,' I said.

His war, as I heard him tell it, was the one you can read about now in books if you care to. I have some of those books near to hand. I've perused them carefully. From many of them, you would think it was just captains and colonels and generals leading each other in one after another handsome charge. There are dates this and battles that. Men were foot soldiers in heaven's war. Quite a healthy number of the women that did get described were saints, and some were angels, hallowed and unscarred. I with my own eyes saw Clara Barton working with the wounded after we fought at Antietam. She brought supplies to the sawbones, gave comfort everywhere she went, and wouldn't quit until she got the typhus and had to be carried away. But there wasn't any saint or angel to it. Just a woman in an apron and a sturdy dress. By the by, she would have looked fierce handsome holding a gun. But there aren't any women holding guns in this pile of books I have. In these stories women are saints and angels and men are courageous noble folk and everything they do gets done nice and quick and nothing smells like blood.

One book talked about Petersburg made it sound like it was a five-minute affair. Like a few officers had set down their cards and whiskey a minute and strolled over out of their mansions and used their officer power to batter down Petersburg's doors. There weren't any Fort Hells or bloody redoubts or gabions or trenches cut for miles in this fellow's telling of it; there weren't any twelve-pounders, no howitzers, no Dictator to smash what bellowed like burning bulls and elephants through the night sky. You would have almost wanted to be there, the way it was told. Let yourself get killed by a bullet to the bosom, let yourself get shot straight up out of your indescribables just to enter the tale. I read it and felt myself mounted up on a charger holding a jousting lance and getting ready to do battle. God and country. Damsels. Shield the children. Mine eyes have seen the glory. Save the poor black brethren. Bathe each night in the light of the stars.

The way Weatherby told it, or the way I heard it, his grandson's fighting for one of the grander Ohio regiments was an awful lot like these books. I hadn't read them yet then, nor had they been written, but they might as well have been. Didn't mean he didn't have his reasons. Maybe they all have their reasons. For telling it like poetry, I mean. I learned this that day when I finally roused myself and spoke.

'You're a nice fellow and you have been kind to me, but it wasn't pretty like the way you're saying it,' I said.

He stopped the wagon when I said this. Pulled on the reins and made the mare snort. A hummingbird buzzed by us and Weatherby gave it a laugh then flicked his stump up sideways in the air. He left his stump pointing straight at the side of my head a minute. The knobbly end of it was browner than any other part of him that I could see.

'They burned that shut with an officer's hand iron,' he said. 'Fifty years ago and I can still feel it. I mentioned earlier I had been to war. It took them four tries, and they had to heat up the iron again between each time. But that's the gentle part of my tale. I know something other than knights in armor about this war we got now. My grandson I'm building this greenhouse for is getting sent home to me next month without half his face and missing both his eyes. You say something one way instead of the other often enough and maybe the thing quits crawling into your bed with you and stroking its claws at your cheek.'

Weatherby said this and then dropped his stump and gave the reins a hard flick. The mare hopped once to the side, then started up again. Weatherby pointed at the air over the road with his chin. The hummingbird was seeing us off. Green shrub. Ruby bloom. We had stopped in its territory. Weatherby had spoken without anything sounded angry in his voice. Only his stump had looked angry. Maybe a fleck or two of the green echoed the hummingbird swimming in his eyes.

'I beg your pardon for misunderstanding you,' I said.

'Isn't any need for begging or pardoning either,' he said.

When we got back to the General's house it was into dusk time and the General's wife was sitting on the front step smoking one of the General's pipes. When I had made my farewells to Weatherby and walked up the front path, she produced a second pipe and we sat a time together there and smoked.

'The General likes to take a walk in the evening with Mr. Weatherby,' she said. 'He finds him fine company.'

'Weatherby likes to talk,' I said.

'When he gets it going.'

'But in a kind way. No argument to it.'

'He is always kind.'

We sat quiet then. If you can call it quiet when the air is getting killed by an army of crickets.

'When will the General come home?' I said.

'When will the war end?' she said. 'In his letters he writes that the fight goes badly. Then he writes that it goes well. Lately, more often it is the latter. Will that bring him home sooner or later? I do not know.'

She said not another word. Our smoke walked out together into the night. After a time I took my pipe up to bed with me. The tobacco was stale but still filled the room with the smell of whiskey and cherry and the fields on which I had fought.

During his speech, Weatherby said his ruined grandson had been at Antietam and I thought about this as I laid my head against the pillows and smoked. Maybe we had both been in the cornfield. Charged nobly forward through the powder smoke. Or maybe his fear had found him and he had turned around and run. Maybe he had been in my madhouse with me before the war had grabbed him back and found a way to steal his face and rip out his eyes.

There must have been some spell to that tobacco I carried up to my room for I spent days entire afterward, didn't matter how hot it was, back down under the covers in the dim, my eye, tearless as it was, sometimes eating at the dust whirling the light planks come in through cracks in the curtains, sometimes the dark of the pillows, sometimes just the back of its own lid. Other days I rose and worked in the garden or saw to the yard or cleaned windows or washed floors from dusk until dawn, smelling the fresh airs of the world all the length of the day, only to crawl at its end back into that room and under those covers where I stopped remembering battles and madhouses and husbands and stories and the soft breath of small babies and mothers who broke their own commands. I did my eating at night, standing in the cool of the pantry. Sometimes the General's wife would come down in her night-gown and stand alongside me and eat her meal that way too. We almost never talked as we ate. Just let our fingers go out and open jars and cut slices and spread spreads. It was one of these nights, as we were eating hoecakes and honey, that she put her hand on my hand and asked me if I was awake or asleep.

'I don't know,' I said, so she told me to follow her and we went out to the pump where she had me fill a bowl and give it to her. Then she lifted up that bowl and poured it over my head.

For a minute I was far away. I was back in the heat of Virginia. I was standing at the General's side. He was asking me to be a sharpshooter; I was hiding in a well; whole days went by as I waited to take my shot, and then I was in a tree, swaying with its branches, leaning with its leaves, aiming my gun. 'I know you didn't steal out of any of your own comrades' haversacks, I know it, you are my sharpshooter, you are my best soldier,' the General said. The bowl came back up off my head before I could answer.

The General's wife told me then as I dripped out there in the yard in Ohio and not on the fighting fields of Virginia that I could stay at her house for as long as I wanted but that it was time to wake now, that I had slept long enough, that there would be sufficient time in the hereafter for the variety of sleeping I had been doing those past weeks.

'Your husband, my General, left me behind to rot in that madhouse,' I said.

'Are you sure that's the way it happened? Are you sure that is what he did?' she said.

I was silent a long time.

'I'm not sure,' I said.

It was the next day I put an end to my thinking and got myself roused up to go. After she had filled my sack with jars and sandwiches, the General's wife walked me to the edge of town. We had a plan to stop by Weatherby's on my way out, for he had built his greenhouse. She said as we walked it was a wide world had new greenhouses go up on one of its ends and black powder to blow a man apart on its other. I said she wasn't wrong. That the world was wide. I had seen some of it. Weatherby had too. We all had. Chasms never greater and miles just as long. She whistled as we walked. It was a handsome tune, happy and mournful both, and I realized I had been hearing it every day the past weeks without listening to it.

'What is that you are whistling?' I asked her.

She looked at me long and a little strange, then laughed. It was just something she had heard from the General when he had last been home on leave, a song his men and lieutenants and captains liked to sing or whistle when they played cards or washed dishes or dressed wounds or cleaned rifles or wrote letters or chopped wood or raised tents or lay in their sickbeds or stood firm by their cannon or mounted their horses or ran into battle for a war wouldn't ever end or wandered the fresh fields of the dead.

'The General sang this song?' I asked.

'Oh, he loved to sing it,' she answered.

'Say its name,' I whispered.

She put her hand on my arm and leaned close to my ear and whispered back.

When we arrived, Weatherby gave us a ceremonial bow and asked after the General. We talked on the General some but it got to sound almost like we were making speeches, one after the other, and we left off. The General's wife had brought Weatherby a few jars of pickled carrots, one of which she opened for him.

'Nothing in the world quite like a pickled comestible to my way of looking at it,' Weatherby said.

'They are choice morsels,' I said.

'You can say it and then you can say it again and not use it up,' he said.

'Show us what you have built,' the General's wife said.

I was ready for the road but found my curiosity for this new thing too strong. Weatherby led us past a wide square of peach trees were now loaded and not above a week away from producing and past the silvery curve of a little stream.

'You got sold smudged glass,' I said when we came to it. It was a pretty thing, planted off by itself in the middle of a fresh-scythed lawn, with the glass neat set, but all the panes I could see from where we stood held marks.

'I got sold what I paid for.' Weatherby smiled strangely. 'Just exactly what I paid for.'

'That's picture glass,' the General's wife said. 'A greenhouse made out of picture ghosts.'

We went inside. Stood among the empty benches. As we watched, the sun tore off its cloud and lit up a hundred likeness images. It was the happy faces of fifty men gone off to war and fifty women didn't. Or maybe they didn't. Maybe there were some standing up there straight in their Sunday dresses were out right that minute on the field holding rifles, getting their arms sawed off, dying over their slops, singing it out with all the rest of them about watch fires and fateful lightning and the coming of the Lord. Away off somewhere in that other country knowing they would never get home. There was ghost pictures too of countryside and farm buildings, a town square, a trail, flowering bushes, a tree in the sunlight, a brook in the breeze. There was even three or four windows full of boys had got left behind in their bones at the Second Bull Run, which the photographer, Weatherby told us, had visited the weeks before he died.

Weatherby and the General's wife stayed inside that greenhouse awhile longer but my face and neck had grown hot, so I stepped outside into the cool and thought I would walk a minute among the peach trees. They were old and intergrown so I had to work and crouch a little to pass between them and after a minute gave it up and sat down near the middle of the orchard against a trunk. There were sweat bees and butterflies at their work and one of them, with green and gold and turquoise to its wing, took my eye over to the back of Weatherby's house, where, sitting on the bench in the sunlight, I saw his grandson. He was wearing pants and undershirt and had his hands in his lap. The hands were big and the fingers skeletal. His bare feet, planted firm in front of him, were flat and narrow and long. There was a clean bandage wrapped around his ears. Over his face he wore a purple veil. There was a little bit of a breeze playing with the under-end of it. Otherwise there wasn't a thing on or around him outside flying insects that moved. He might have been graven. Image of hurt for the ages. Hurt come home. I stood after a minute and started to crouch my way out of the orchard to give him a good morning, but my feet found out other ideas and before I knew it I was off and away, without any farewells, let alone good mornings, on my road.

I thought as I put Yellow Springs behind me and walked fast away that it was seeing those dead soldiers and that whole world being lit to vanishing that made me want even harder than I had to get home before it was too late and Bartholomew and I and the wide world got turned to just some jelly dried to a cracked glass sheet. Cracked for the wind to whistle through. I thought too it might be the picture that bloomed up of Weatherby's blind grandson tending sprouts in his purple veil under all those fading faces he couldn't see, all those eyes fading off away until they were all as blind as he was that had put the snap in my step and made me move. Or maybe it was just the smell I still had in my nose of pickled carrots and the sound in my ears of them being crunched by Weatherby with his old teeth in that quiet place. Or the after-hum I had in my head of the General's wife whistling 'The Ballad of Gallant Ash.'

Whatever it was, I walked away and didn't stop any longer than I had to over those last miles. So much so that it wasn't much more than a week after I'd left them at their floating room and its ghosts that I walked back up into Randolph County where I'd left from better than two years before. It was late. Raining, or I would have pushed on for home that evening. Instead, I spent a night with some boys had a fire going under a rubber sheet rigged up high next to a field near Winchester. They had three women with them who all looked happy enough. The boys were back from the war, is what they said, and the women had come out to meet them. They were having a party out of the homecoming and there were jugs of corn whiskey involved.

I took my drink and shared out what I had left of the jars and sandwiches from the General's wife and we had a fine old time. They had some impressive firearms they'd brought back with them, including a pair of Sharps and a Henry breech-loader made me give out a whistle. That whistle led to a firing demonstration once the rain had stopped. The Henry looked like it had come straight out of the crate and into their hungry arms. It could hit any size object you liked at any distance

219

if you knew how to shoot it. Which I knew I could and which the fellow who said he owned it could not. After he had made the dirt around the can do some high kicks, I took my turn and showed how it was done. I had my suspicions about whether or not those boys had done much soldiering when they couldn't answer straight about where they had been and had fought and just which line they had stood in to fire off fine fresh weapons like the ones they were toting, but my mind was mostly elsewhere up the road. It was elsewhere enough that when later the boy that claimed to own the Henry left off trying on his snoring woman and climbed on top of me, I let him go with a kick and a elbow to his jaw.

He crawled back over to his woman and set in to snoring next to her and I thought I'd try to join the party but I couldn't fall asleep. I lay there under the Indiana stars and thought my thoughts. Couldn't quit thinking them. Not too far off dawn, my paramour let off a loud fart, woke himself up with it, and came back over at me. I was agitated and hit him down harder than I probably would otherwise have done.

This got the whole band of them roused and before I knew it I was getting chased a hundred yards down the road. Later that same morning, just ahead of noontime, I stepped my foot back down on the dirt of my farm.

I didn't do much more than step on it before I left out again. Off yonder in my yard I had spied the fat criminal I'd known all my life called Big Ned Phipps feeding hay to geldings I'd never seen before in a corral I hadn't built. The seed shed was burned to the ground, the mule pen was empty, and some of our fence was knocked down. There wasn't any crop to speak of in the field, and a dozen ugly goats were snapping at each other and nibbling the weeds. Here and there around the yard there were holes had been dug in my dirt. Close up next to the house there were four boys sitting in the shade holding plates in their hands. They were laughing and leaning back on our chairs. They were the good chairs, not the ones we used for sitting together in the yard. They had been my mother's and hers that loved roses before that. Two of them sitting there in the mud on my good chairs had been off to war and come back before I'd left home. One was the son-of-a-bitch who'd pushed me down at the market when I was a girl and who I'd gone back and fought in my muddy dress until he cried, and the other I had never seen before.

After a time one of them hollered into the house and the next minute my Bartholomew came out. He was holding a tray had cups of coffee on it. He went around to each of the boys and let them choose a cup. By and by Big Ned called for his and Bartholomew went over and stood there a long time in the June sun as Ned moved his mouth and made a fuss over picking it up. I came a tongue crunch away from calling out at Bartholomew to crack that cup of coffee over Ned Phipps's head but if there is one thing war and the lunatic house can teach you it is how to wait.

I walked five miles back the way I had come from that morning and I climbed into the cool under some mulberry bushes and I slept. I woke around nightfall and waited until it was late and the moon had dropped down into its cradle of earth. Then I went back to the sleeping camp of boys and their women and stepped right into the middle of it and plucked up a box of cartridges and the Henry gun. They must have all gone swimming down at the creek because they were snoring there in their wet underthings. The one had tried his luck with me was about my size. It took me a long minute of groping but when I left, I had his hat on my head and his clothes under my arm.

I walked a mile or two east under the stars, then cut north another mile and bivouacked under a shag-bark hickory looked about set to fall down. I tried sleeping some but didn't. At first light I took a good look at the Henry. They had mishandled it doing their dirt designs but the mechanism was still true. I took it apart, cleaned it as best I could, put it back together again. I removed my dress and wrapped the Henry

222

in it and hid it under some brush a hundred feet from the hickory. Then I again changed my clothes. The pants were big but I found myself some rope. The outfit smelled ripe but I reckoned that helped my cause.

Town was just waking up when I walked in. I stepped straight into the café and ordered coffee and biscuits. I had ordered that same thing regular in that same café all the grown years of my life but I was in my other clothes and they could not see me. When I had eaten I called over for more coffee.

'You been off to the fight,' said the can of corned beef brought it over and couldn't recognize me.

I nodded. Said I'd had my discharge. Said I was passing through on my way home.

'Home where?' he said. He had leaned against the counter and crossed his arms, interested in the traveler going his way from somewhere to somewhere else.

I pointed out through the wall in the direction more or less of Marion and Noblesville. I took a sip of my coffee. Took a look at my fingernails, picked out a speck of grime.

'I paid a visit to a farm about three miles yonder yesterday evening, looking to beg a sup of water and some directions, found the welcome wasn't any too warm,' I said.

'Which farm was that?' he said.

'Horse farm, to look at it. They've had some fire trouble and fence damage. Goats grazing wild and such.'

The man uncrossed his arms and gave out a laugh.

'That's what used to be the Thompson farm. Gal and her husband. Gal ran off and joined the gypsies. Little fellow she left behind couldn't fend off the wolves.'

'I heard some of those wolves are Secesh lovers.'

'I couldn't speak to that.'

'I saw a little corncob serving them cups of coffee.'

'Bartholomew Thompson. He's missing the fight because of a bad foot or eyes or some such. Boys that took his farm let him run their errands and live in the barn.'

I took another sip of my coffee. I looked the man in the eye a good while. He had aged but a little, had a few fresh wrinkles and only just a bit more yellow in his eye than before. He wasn't any thinner than he had been either.

'Sounds like he could have used a hand in the fight. I expect there's folks love the Union in the vicinity.'

If he heard the iron in my voice he didn't show it.

'Time of war,' he said. 'I reckon there's more want him gone than want him to stay.'

'You among them?'

It was his turn to give me a good look.

'I reckon whether I am or I'm not isn't any of your affair, stranger.'

We talked war and devils for a while and by the time I left I decided I had had the answer to my question and didn't need to pursue it further. My next stop was the sheriff's office. The man who had put his boot on the neck of that institution for many a year and who had stood shouting amongst the burning-out crowd two weeks before my mother hung herself one rainy morning from the ash tree on the edge of our farm was cousin to Ned Phipps, but the fellow built like a broke-string banjo I talked to there told me that old outlaw had gotten drunk one night the past winter before investigating some pranks at the rail yard and let a train take off his legs. They had him in a rolling chair up at the county home. This man, his successor, had only an unrifled musket in his arsenal to go with his badge and wasn't going to gun for anyone took an angry interest in Ned Phipps.

'Where you heading off to?' he said when I walked back out of his sorry door.

'Home. Home is where I'm goddamn heading,' I said.

On my way out of town and back to the Henry I passed the very Ned Phipps I had business with. He was riding one of the horses he kept corralled on my property. Riding it grand like the cavalry officer he had never been. It was a crow-black racing horse about as handsome as they come. You could see it was on its way to having its back broken by the fat son-of-a-bitch sitting like a general on top of it. That fat son-of-a-bitch gave me down a green-toothed smile and a nod.

'You back from the fight?' he said.

'Traveling to it,' I said.

'Well, then, I wish you luck.'

In my dream of it there is no moon and there are no stars and I am lost in a crowd carrying torches to set the world alight. My mother's voice and I cannot reach her. My mother's voice farther away or me from it as the crowd grows closer and closer still. They turn giant and I rain my blows against their giant legs.

'Constance,' my mother calls out in the dream. Her voice sounds as thin as a piece of paper and twice as light. 'Constance, come and stand up here beside me.' But in the dream I am afraid. In the dream I turn my back on my mother and run.

On that night it was different from the dream. We had heard there was to be trouble at the house of our neighbor the woman whose husband was gone and who had her two babies and nothing else but the peeling paper on her walls to protect her. My mother sent me to my room to sleep and told me to shut my eyes, but they stayed open and I climbed out my window as soon as I knew she had gone. There was stars and moon aplenty, in the memory and not the dreams, and I could see her up ahead stepping her long legs through the barley. There was a crowd of them already there and my mother walked straight through that crowd and went to stand on the neighbor woman's front step and face them. She crossed her strong arms over her chest and yelled out to them that they needed to head home and look to their own business. Leave women and their babies alone. She had just yelled this a second time when I came through the crowd and climbed up the steps and stood next to her. In the house behind us the neighbor woman was sitting at her kitchen table with a babe in each arm. Her eyes were wild and she was singing a song I'd never heard before. Rocking a little on a chair wasn't a rocker. There was upward of fifty of them holding their torches and stepping ever closer to the house and setting in to jeer.

'We don't ever turn our cheek, do we, Mama?' I said and crossed my own arms and looked out at the crowd. The constable was at the front of it. Ned Phipps, who I had known of since I was five years old, was there. There was a woman in the mob holding a pitchfork and yelling out for the others to toss forward their torches and send us and all the gypsy niggers in the house to hell.

'No, we don't,' my mother said and as she said this, her voice cracked. It was just a speck of a crack, the smallest thing, like a twig touched in winter, but I had never heard any crack come out of her throat before. I looked up and saw there were tears on her cheeks and that her lower lip was moving. A minute later she had set off away, first at a fast walk, then at a run. When she had left I found I couldn't keep my arms crossed.

They dangled at my sides like they'd been sawed down to the strings. Still, it was me helped the neighbor woman to leave, who took one of the babes and a bundle and walked her away through the crowd already set into their burning and off a long stretch down the road. When we got close to the Ohio border, about where I would cross it again those years later on my way to war, she told me I better get back and see to my mother, that whether she would confess to it or not, she was the one needed seeing to now.

'But where will you go?' I said, for she looked small and alone with her children and her bundle there on the midnight road.

'You go on now, go on back home,' she said.

I followed after her awhile but she would not speak to me any longer, was already striding away from Indiana and off into the sadness of the world. World woven from the wool of such partings.

My mother and I did not speak about that night on any of the days that followed even though the cinders of what had been the neighbor woman's house smoked dark and slow through every one. I kept looking for my mother to find a piece of fine story to put onto the end of this poor one but she stayed quiet and no crown of justice came to her brow, no sword of vengeance crept into her hand.

A week or ten days into this some boys on horses called of an evening at the edge of our property. They had a torch with them might have been one from that night. Any other time my mother would have seen them off like sick sparrows but she just sat crumpled at the kitchen table and it was me had to walk out to the edge of the property with her musket and back them down.

'Your fear will find you out someday too, daughter mine. It will find you out and use its wiles and crinkle your heart,' she said when I came in and put the musket down. I bit my lip. Did not answer. I knew it was true. She seemed to rouse herself some after she had said this. We worked at blade sharpening and spilled out some good sweat together in the yard. Bartholomew came over with another flower and my mother heated us up a jar of ham and green beans. 'That's a good boy you got ahold of there,' she said. She let me walk him halfway back to his house and he kissed me a minute in a ditch beside the fencerow. That night my mother told me the story about the princess and the dragon only at the end of the story it was the princess cut off the dragon's head. It may be that Bartholomew had come back and was crouched outside the window and giving a listen. 'Good night,' my mother said to me when she had finished. She touched my arm and held it when she said this. Later it was more than one time I would look down at my arm and think I could see a mark she had left in touching me. Who is to say that's just folly? Who is to say what it is we have left on us after we have been touched? There is the world with its night-walking women and then there is what happens in it. A few days later my mother climbed up into the ash tree with a rope.

I do not know why it was this I chose to speak of that evening after dark when I had retrieved the Henry and put my dress back on and climbed up into the hayloft of our barn and found my Bartholomew lying under a horse blanket in the straw. I had not stood near him in two years that could have been twenty but when I leaned in close to his face and woke him, it was my mother I spoke of, my mother and her fear and her hand on my arm, her hand on my arm more than anything, and the neighbor woman walking off with her children, and my mother's death in the ash tree. Bartholomew tried to speak more than once while I was talking but I did not let him. When I had finished I told him that the next morning early he needed to get down to the house and fetch my mother's old musket and see it was charged and bring it to me. Then he was to go back down and put his apron on and serve all the boys their morning coffee in the yard. When they all of them had their coffee he was to go back inside the house and not come out. No matter what he heard. They had tried to take our land and used him poorly and spoken for Secession and now it was their turn to be used. It was simple. Simplest thing in the world. Simple as standing and not running. Walking with the turn of the earth instead of against it. He was to listen to me. I said this twice. He was not to disobey.

'Let me speak,' he said.

I did not answer. There was blood already dripping from

230

my lips and my eyes and he did not open his mouth again, only looked at me a little queer, like he had seen his dream of me gone mad come now to crouch above him, and nodded when I repeated myself. Then I told him I was done talking and called him husband and made him lie back down.

Sleep without dream. Tunnel without end. Sky without stars. Rainbows burst to bloody colored bits. I did not know where I was when I woke and I stumbled around in the straw for a minute, imagined there was chained women sleeping around me, that there was minié bullets or a bucket of ice water and fists coming for my head. I told Bartholomew, who wasn't there, not to fret, that we would fight the keeper and her ice bucket off together. Then I heard voices in the yard. I picked up the Henry, fed it all the way full of cartridges, and went to the hayloft window. It was still some dark out but you could smell sun in the purple sky and I could cipher well enough. Men in the yard. Metal in their hands. They were wearing hats and long coats against the morning cold and they were bunched and smeared together. It took me the only several seconds I had but I counted first four, then all five of them.

They had the barn to their front, the house behind, and forty fine yards on either side. It was like the door had been shut on them. Like when those boys got caught down in the crater and couldn't climb up its sides. I didn't like what I was about to set to doing, but I didn't like them spending their days setting there on my chairs worse. I didn't like

Bartholomew fetching them their coffee worse. I didn't like the deep fat on the back of Ned Phipps who some said was my father either. Ned Phipps who some said was my father who had helped scare off my mother and burn out our neighbor woman worse. It was him I shot first. I breathed and then hit him on the side of the neck and he fell out of his boots like a side of bad beef and went crawling off in the direction of his horse. The one I had fought with at the market took his in the forehead. The bullet stove out the back of his head and left a spray in the dawn light almost up to the house. The three of them left unhit needed to move but instead stood staring at Ned crawling off and at the boy had once troubled me now dead as dust sitting on the dirt beside them. I shot another twice in his chest and then into the middle of my fury came a goat up out of nowhere, crazed and hopping left and right, so I shot it too. It sat back on its haunches then folded up its front legs and dripped down its head.

When the goat went down the other two boys took it as a sign and dropped the guns they hadn't once fired, cried mercy, went into squats and put their hands over their heads. At the minute they did this I heard a hard creak behind me and turned a little and saw a hat and a gun barrel coming up the hole into the shadow of the haymow. The hat came up and the gun lifted after it and I spun full around and shot as the black circle of the barrel found my face. I took the climber through his shoulder and he slumped over and set the gun down gentle in the straw.

Boys had been squatting outside started to run at my shot and I took the one trailing a step straight through his side. I would have taken out the last a short second later only the Henry jammed. I gave a quick try at clearing the mechanism but it wouldn't budge and I saw the boy wasn't shot running past Ned Phipps toward the corral. I didn't like to be too rough but the one had tried to come up behind me was blocking my way so after I had grabbed up his gun I shoved him down the ladder. He hit barn dirt with a whump and groan. I was over him and out the side door when I saw what the son-of-a-bitch had meant to end my days with: I now had my mother's musket in my hand.

Old weapon. Built for other fights and days. It hadn't ever been rifled and wobbled its round balls like drunk babies but I could see even at a run that it had been well oiled and I knew that it would hit. The boy was already bareback on Ned Phipps's handsome black horse and had the corral open when I came around the barn. He reined up a minute when he saw who it was in her skirts had been shooting at them. Just like that outlaw boy had done in the house in the woods. I didn't say a word, only kept coming forward the way we had been taught in the Kentucky fields, the way we had done it in the Maryland pasture, the way we had fought with the cannon fire killing us into wet nothing in the Virginia woods. I kept coming so he kicked the horse hard and cleared the corral and lit out down the road toward town. I got my line of sight, kneeled, lifted my mother's musket, lowered it a quarter inch, let out my breath, fired off my wobbly ball through the dawn, and shot him down. The handsome black horse galloped on a ways without its rider, then stopped, gave itself a shake, and set in to nibbling like it was Sunday afternoon. I had no urge to shoot at it. The goat had been a mistake. I felt bad about that goat and would not murder a horse.

Ned Phipps was gurgling loud over at the corral fence. He had got about halfway up to standing. His hat had fallen off and his pants had slid loose down his legs in the crawling. When I got up on him he was dead. Father mine. The others in the yard were just as finished or aiming fast for it.

'Come on out now, Bartholomew,' I called. I got no answer. Called again. I looked at the musket in my hands, then I counted the corpses. My heart skipped a hard beat so I counted again. Five dead boys and a goat. The one inside made it six. Six was too many.

Before he died with his head in my lap at the bottom of the barn ladder where I had thrown him, Bartholomew asked me what it had been like down south at the war, and I told him it had been hot.

'It was hot here too, Constance, and I thought you were dead,' he said.

'Then, husband, you have been kissed and shot by a ghost.'

'I wanted to sell,' he said. 'Sell and move on out of here. I lacked only the deed.'

'You could have done it without the deed. All you had to do was take their money.'

'I wanted to do it right.'

'You would have never found it.'

'I'd've kept digging.'

'You were my one true love; you put feathers in my letters, you left me a lilac bundle by my breakfast in the long ago.'

'Was I?'

'Always.'

'Every day I took up the shovel and dug for the deed. Ned made me a fair offer. He and his boys were helping me dig.

There wasn't any harm in it. You didn't have to kill them all. You should have stayed down there a little longer at your war.'

'And you should have looked up into the trees, husband, not down into the dirt.'

'You hid it in the ash tree,' he said.

'Yes,' I said.

Then he died.

The scrawny sheriff was in his office, and when I told him I was Constance Thompson returned from my wayfaring, he said he had just that minute come back from my land. I started to make my speech and ask for my noose but he stopped me, gave me his condolences, told me my farm had been the site of a terrible crime. Once more I started in on my speech and once more he stopped me. He said a stranger had been in town asking questions about our farm. The stranger had been at the café and complained about some slight of hospitality out our way. The stranger, said the scrawny sheriff, was fresh back from the war and had had nothing but blood in his eyes. The last anyone had seen of this stranger was when he had walked out of town heading our way. You could put that all together. The other part to the equation, he went on, was that there had been some boys and a posse of flouncy women camping and carrying on out in the hinterlands had come into town sniffling about a missing Henry repeater rifle. They had told some that they had been in the war and others that they hadn't but they had clammed up tight, and left soon after, when someone asked just how they had come to lose such a gun.

'You see any blood in these eyes I'm looking at you with?' I asked the sheriff when he was done telling me everything I already knew.

'You have had quite a shock and look road-weary and I will see to your husband's arrangements if you like, madam,' is what he said.

'I killed them all, every one, even my Bartholomew,' I said.

'You will want to rest up now, Mrs. Thompson,' said the sheriff. 'I will have a buckboard take you back home.'

'Take who home? There's more than one of me here,' I aid.

Before Bartholomew breathed his last I let his head down soft onto the dirt floor of the barn and I went out to the edge of the south field and climbed the ash tree where my mother had hung herself and where I had found her swinging on the last day of my youth. I climbed it and felt for the notch just above the branch where she had tied her rope. In the notch was an oilskin bag and in the bag was the deed to my farm. I brought the deed down out of the tree and I carried it into the barn.

'You want to sell, we'll sell, there's other buyers in the world,' I said to my Bartholomew. 'We can move off away elsewhere. Make a new start. Try for a family together again.'

But he was already dead.

Not so long ago I was coming back from a trade show and passed a greenhouse made of glass from photographic plates. It was bigger but not better built than Weatherby's, and it had been made along the same lines. This one had been standing some time when I saw it and all that was left of what the glass had shown was smudges of gray, swirls of brown. The woman had the greenhouse said it was a company out of Pennsylvania had built it for her. She said it had been pretty when they had put it up and the images had given off just the right speck of shade but now the sun had had its way and all the ladies and soldiers she had liked to look at were gone. I got the name of the company before I left and wrote them when I got home but they had gone out of business and said they couldn't help me.

It took me a while but I tracked down three plates of that kind of glass in a likeness shop over in Lafayette and put them in our kitchen window here on the farm. Two fine ladies and one man. Spring and summer, the morning light catches them there, lights them each a minute out of their darkness, lets them glow. One morning these past weeks, as I was looking at them, there was a knock on my door. It was a woman dressed in plain clothes and scuffed shoes about my age had come to pay me a call. She had dust on her from the road and when I asked her she told me she was up from near Yellow Springs, Ohio, so I let her in. We drank hot tea at the kitchen table next to the fading pictures. She was housekeeper to a friend of the General and his wife and at one of the dinners she had helped serve, she had heard a story about a woman had fought for the Union army under the General's command.

'He was a colonel when I fought for him,' I said.

'I did some soldiering myself, or a kind of it,' she said.

I looked a long while at her and she at me. I had never met another since that time on the road with the colored woman had put her knee to my chest, and I had wondered about it, like I expect all of us had put on pants and gone to war did.

'What made you go?' I said, facing away from her.

'There was two of us,' I heard her say. 'It was the other one of us put on the colors. I just kind of rode along.'

'Do you smoke a pipe?' I said.

She said she did and we stepped outside and sat on my front steps and smoked a pipe and traded stories of our adventures in the war. I spoke first and said not very much at all, though it seemed to satisfy her. When it came her turn she told me that her name during the war had been Leonidas and that her friend's name had been Leander. Leonidas and Leander had been together through the whole long days of the fight.

'We had started out,' she told me, 'hauling wood and

240

tending stock and working in the fields in place of all the boys who had gone. When we got tired of that and of our harping parents, we followed after them and saw the bullets fly and heard the cannons roar. We went out onto the fields after the fighting and walked among the dead men and helped take them to their graves. We saw the surgeries where the men were brought to have their limbs removed. We watched them chop a boy's leg off and throw what they took straight out the front door.'

Dressed in pants, she said, they had attended a battle, and when it went bad and they had killed up most of our side, Leander had put on a dead boy's uniform and took up his firearm and marched away barefoot with the rest of them. Leonidas had followed Leander through all the weeks and months that followed and even though she had not worn a uniform she had many a time lifted up pistol or rifle and brought the hammer down. After one battle, Leander had got thrown in a prison camp and starved and fooled with and beat for kicking in the teeth of the someone who had fooled with her. Leonidas had met Leander at the gate when they got tired of her troublemaking and set her free.

'She wouldn't speak a word when she left that evil place and so we walked the roads until she one day got her voice back. "Now, that was something and, goddamn, that was something, and goddamn all of it to hell" is what she said.'

Leander had made this comment as they were walking through a pine forest. Every step in that forest had lifted up

241

something soft and special to smell. You could, Leonidas told me as we sat smoking on my steps, have just laid down on that ground and gone right to sleep or died.

'But we didn't die yet and there we went a-walking. We turned a corner and come upon a pool of water. When we stepped up close to drink we saw it was shallow and full of dead crickets. Leander looked at those crickets and the tears came climbing up. "Every one of them is dead," she said. We cried and cried.'

As they were returning home at last by paddleboat, Leander was taken by a fever and had joined the crickets, along with a number of others. The paddleboat captain, fearing further infection, had organized a burial party on a sandbar. Leonidas had tried as best she could to mark the spot but when she returned some while later she found nothing of her friend but the wide waters of the river. As for her subsequent life without Leander she remarked, 'I made it back, sure enough, but never felt I'd made it home.'

In the days following this visit, which ended very soon after those last words, I wrote a letter down to Yellow Springs, to the General, to tell him that it was true that I had stolen food out of haversacks, that I was sorry for it and did not know why I had done it and wished I could put all that food I had stolen and eaten back. That maybe things would have turned out different and for the better if I had done so. Leonidas had asked me not to speak of her in any communication with the General, so instead I asked after Weatherby and

Weatherby's grandson and the General's wife and told the General to send them all my regards.

My husband was long since deceased, I wrote him. By my own hand. I had seen him garbed but not disguised in cloak and hat and climbing up the ladder carrying my mother's musket, and I had grown frightened – of what had been and what was there – and had seen him in my mind's eye taking aim at me with it, even though he had not taken aim at me, and I had shot him.

He comes to me sometimes, I wrote. He comes and sits with me at my table or stands in my doorway after I've had one of my bad dreams or goes walking out on some business across the yard. I try to talk to him but he will not talk to me. Only sits or stands there. Not all things disappear quickly.

It was a long letter. I included in it too an apology that when the General had come to see me in the lunatic house, I had unbuttoned my dress and made to sit in his lap. I apologized for having scratched his face and hit him with the vase of flowers at the start of his visit and for having cursed him to his grave when he shoved me away. I told him I had since tried to do better but had not always done better.

Fear finds you out, I wrote. It always finds you out.

I have not had any answer yet.

# Acknowledgments

*Neverhome* could not have come into being without the help and support of Linda K. Wickens, Susan Schulten, Susie Schlesinger, Susan Manchester, Kathryn Hunt, Selah Saterstrom, Eva Sikelianos Hunt, K. Allison Wickens, Harry Mathews, Anna Stein, Chris Fischbach, Josh Kendall, Nicole Dewey, Miriam Parker, Pamela Marshall, Garrett McGrath, and Eleni Sikelianos (always). Profound thanks also to the Lannan Residency Program in Marfa, Texas.

A few of the many excellent works I consulted during the writing of *Neverhome* deserve special mention: *Dearest Susie: A Civil War Infantryman's Letters to His Sweetheart* by Frank Ross McGregor; *The Civil War Notebook of Daniel Chisholm,* edited by W. Springer Menge and J. August Shimrak; *Turned Inside Out: Recollections of a Private Soldier in the Army of the Potomac* by Frank Wilkeson; *The Slaves' War* by Andrew Ward; *This Republic of Suffering: Death and the American Civil War* by Drew Gilpin Faust; *They Fought Like Demons: Women Soldiers in the Civil War* by DeAnne Blanton and

Lauren M. Cook; and, most crucially, *An Uncommon Soldier: The Civil War Letters of Sarah Rosetta Wakeman, Alias Private Lyons Wakeman, 153rd Regiment, New York State Volunteers, 1862–1864* by Lauren Cook Burgess.

The *Southern Landscapes* and battlefield photographs of Sally Mann were indispensable in helping me travel with Ash through mid-nineteenth-century America, as were the first two *New History Warfare* albums of Colin Stetson and the song 'Sorrow, Sorrow' by Lorna Hunt.